Bound Through Blood

Alexis Kennedy

Books by Alexis Kennedy

Bound Through Blood

Under the Blood Moon (Hearts on Fire Book 1)

Ravaged (Dial M for Murder Book 1)

Déjà Vu (Dial M for Murder Book 2)

Cupid (Dial M for Murder Book 3)

Two Faced

Scandalous

Angry House

Birthright (Destiny Bound Book 1)

Indelible (Two Faced book 2)

Gods and Angels

Lycan Moon (Hearts on Fire Book 2)

Deadly Games (Elusive Killers Book 1)

"Books are just dreams in print."
~Alexis Kennedy

For my mother because she taught me to love vampire stories.

Prologue

Louisiana colony 1720

Devin was a taker; he took what he wanted without asking, ever. He was a predator and a master of seduction. But then a day came when something was taken from him—his heart.

Lovelier than any woman Devin had hunted before, her fair skin—curtained by silky black hair and adorned with sparkling blue eyes that made the clearest sky jealous—tugged at his willpower. She was such a rare beauty with her exquisite delicateness; it was impossible to take his eyes off her.

Devin watched her all that night and the next day before he approached her. She was as unable to resist him as centuries of women before her had been. But, unlike those other women, she was not the evening's fare—she had become his heart's desire. Her destiny was to be bound to him through blood. She'd become his savior—she had the power to return him to a mortal existence. But the colonists had decided otherwise and took his chance at life and his love away from him.

New Orleans, Louisiana—May 2013

Devin was hungry; it had been two days since he'd fed his thirst. He'd been wandering around the Midwest, but something drew him back here almost three centuries later. He didn't think he'd ever walk these grounds again—his place of pain; his own personal hell—yet here he was, and the night wound around him as he crept through its shadows in search of his prey.

It was dark outside the building he surveyed, but a single light coming out of a third-story window caught his attention. He saw a buxom blond pass by the window and knew she was tonight's feast. He waited until the light was out.

Madison stirred from her sound sleep when a strange sensation overcame her. The room felt hot, even though she had the ceiling fan on and the window open, and it was hard to breathe. Her instincts revealed to her, though, that it wasn't the muggy air making her breath come in short gasps; she had the distinct impression she was no longer alone in her room. At first, she thought her roommate must have returned, but then she got goosebumps as a pleasant, musky fragrance reached her.

Frightened, Madison searched the shadows, trying to adjust her eyes. Then the clouds gave way to the full moon, and it outlined a large shape at the foot of her bed.

She knew she should scream, but something stopped her—an unexpected paralyzing excitement— something to do with the fragrance. She breathed in the unfamiliar musk and let it wash over her senses and pet her intimately. Intoxicated, she felt drawn to the mysterious shape. She slowly climbed from her bed, and her white filmy nightgown clung to her voluptuous body from perspiration. Hesitating, she approached the shape, which now encouraged her with a velvety, deep, and hypnotic voice.

"That's right. Come to me."

As she approached the figure, excitement burrowed deep and hot inside her, and she found out that he was larger than she'd first thought. He was well over six feet tall, had sexy broad shoulders—curtained by long, dark hair—and he filled the tiny room. He was wearing a white shirt, black pants, and a smile—a menacing but intoxicating smile that taunted and teased her—there was something she couldn't put her finger on about that smile. Again, she knew she should be frightened, but she couldn't move away and couldn't look away.

He stared into her eyes and slowly took strands of her blond hair between his fingers.

She purred with expectation.

He let his fingertips glide from the edge of her delicate shoulder to her neck and caressed it, lingering over her pulse. As he did so, he felt her heartbeat quicken; yes, he had her now. He leaned in to slowly kiss her lips.

She felt a heat encompass her and tried to deepen the kiss, needing to have more of him.

The force of Devin's resolve restrained her. Not too much too soon, he wanted this to be perfect and under his total control.

She moaned from her frustration, and he replied with a low throaty laugh at her innocence. The laugh surprised her, but her lips didn't hesitate; she needed this stranger. Madison hungered for him, and it was obvious between her milky white thighs; she felt her silky panties dampen and cling to her swollen mound. She'd never done this with a stranger before, but a magnetic force was pulling her toward him, and she was helpless to fight it. The entranced woman reached up to touch him, but in a movement too quick for her to comprehend under her haze, he grabbed her wrists and restrained them behind her back. It should have scared her, but something about it was so arousing, she simply sighed.

Madison looked into his eyes—mysterious black eyes—the color of a starless night. They touched her in intimate places and sent an electric tingle through her fervent body. Again, he smiled that seductive, peculiar smile. She couldn't pull her eyes away from his perfect lips and teeth—it was his teeth—they were different. His teeth were much sharper looking than they should be. She should be terrified…

He claimed her lips again with more urgency this time, wanting to prepare her. He trailed slow movements along her jawline and cascaded down her neck. The pause over her strong, steady pulse took much restraint—he hungered. It would be too easy to feed that hunger and leave as if he'd never been there. But this woman, this night, was different. He wanted to feed another appetite as well. A lingering memory of what it would be like to relish that former life again summoned him, and his groin responded to the heated call. His sharp senses noticed the welcoming moisture at the apex of her legs. It'd been so long since he'd savored, felt, and pleasured a woman.

Devin slowed his trail of heated kisses as he marveled in his distant memories of what pleasures a woman's body could bring. He knew no woman could deny him if she had tried. There was no reason to reach between her legs to know that this one didn't want to try—yet he did. While continuing the blazing path down her neck, once again pausing at the welcoming pulse, he let his free hand slide down her waist and over her hips to take its rest underneath her nightgown. She was wet, so incredibly wet, and her lips were full and swollen for him. She released such a wonderful sigh as he began to tease her pink jewel. Her moisture made the movements easy. He worked her bud in slow circles, feeling it harden more and more under his expert touch. He let go of her wrists, so his other hand was free to clutch her buttocks. He pushed her deeper onto his probing fingers, which were now slipping between her petals.

She gasped and grabbed his shoulders with urgent desire. Her body yielded to his touch, begging for more. All her senses were on fire.

He caressed and kneaded her softness one last moment before thrusting a finger into her restless body. His flesh joined with heat, moisture, and pure need. Her muscles convulsed around him, making him groan from his own desires. While his finger moved around inside her, exploring her pleasure point, his thumb continued to torment and pet her swollen bud. His own obvious desire pressed against her, feeding her frenzied passion, while his most urgent hunger grew and put his mouth back into action. He pressed on past her neck to a spot above the top of her gown. Tired of having her body concealed from him, he removed his hands from her flesh and ripped the gown in half, making it fall to the floor.

She should have been shocked at how easily he tore her clothing, but the fire burned through her in an all-consuming frenzy. "More," she whispered.

His only reply was to take a dusky crest into his mouth, suckling and savoring—and she thought even biting.

Pain shot through her, but she couldn't think to react under the blaze of passion engrossing her body.

His finger took its place back inside her, and the exquisite torture continued. When she reached out to encompass his iron-hard tumescence in her small hands, he swept her up and carried her to the bed. He lay her out in her full naked form and slid on top of her.

She clutched at his clothing in an eager attempt to get him naked and receive his pulsating rod inside her before she burst from the heat. With a movement too quick for her to comprehend, his clothes were gone. His body was astounding. She marveled at the perfection of his rippling musculature, thinking he must be a god. The moonlight glistened off his steely contours and amazing male form, causing her eyes to widen from lust at the sight of his virile masculinity—he was much larger than anyone she'd ever experienced before, and she was suddenly shy.

Devin caught her look of modesty and began distracting her from her concerns by working his mouth down the length of her body.

A moan of ecstasy escaped her lips as his mouth trailed down to the delicate softness between her trembling thighs. His skillful mouth moved over all the parts his hand had once been and caused a current of feminine essence to flow from her.

He allowed the nectar to trickle down her thigh before he could no longer contain his appetite. He bit into her sweet, glazed flesh, and the warm blood flowed into his starved mouth.

She cried out at the pain and surprise from the puncture, but she couldn't fight against her passionate trance. Her head spun, trying to make sense of why she couldn't scream, couldn't try to run away. Her body was wracked with overwhelming spasms of sweet release from the expertise of his mouth when it, once again, returned to torment her slippery cleft.

Not wanting it to be over without his other craving being met, he moved from her quivering mound up her body.

She squirmed underneath him, expecting what would come next, and he fulfilled her wish with a long, powerful thrust into her molten passage. Explosions of light flashed behind her eyes as she experienced pleasure like never before.

His hips flexed to bring her passion crested gratification, over and over, while his mouth sought the soft flesh of her full breast.

Again, she felt the pain of liquid fire as his teeth sunk into her. Again, she felt her warm blood seeping out into his eager mouth. *Why?* She couldn't voice the question; yet, she didn't even care. She wanted this, needed this, and craved this. She was suddenly overcome with listlessness, and her eyes fluttered briefly before they closed a final time—la petite mort, *the little death,* indeed.

Devin, while shifted into a large black wolf, paced the woods and recalled the previous night. He could still taste the sweet blood in his mouth, and his groin recalled the other morsel he had allowed himself to sample. His lusty thoughts made him hungry and thick again for both.

He briefly wondered if anyone had found the pretty blond yet, not that it would matter. He had remained a secret for almost seven hundred years because the bite marks he left behind faded rapidly—it was part of his disguise. Sure, there were voodoo priestesses who spoke of the damned, and there were even vampire tours right there in New Orleans, but where was the *real* proof? Who really believed? Killing wasn't ever personal, it was just his life—well, it was his *existence*. The evil existed because he did.

Wondering where to find his next treat, he shifted back into human form and headed out into the evening. The sun was starting to go down over the horizon, and he laughed at the tales that claimed vampires couldn't be in the sunlight. They, or at least he, simply preferred the night—the quiet, the smells, the shadows, the seduction of the darkness and the moon. Since he had picked out the sexy blond last time, he decided he'd try a sultry brunette or redhead next—*variety was the spice of life, right?* He entered a nearby tavern and instantly spotted his meal. It didn't matter that the petite redhead had a man close to her or that his hand was placed possessively on the small of her back. Men weren't an obstacle for him. They actually made his conquests more fun. He would have the man for dessert, but male blood didn't sit well with him. He liked estrogen-rich, feminine blood; it was much sweeter to the taste.

When he caught sight of her aroused peaks showing through the gauzy top she was wearing, desire thickened him, so there was that matter to take care of as well. Dangling between her perky breasts was a crucifix, so perhaps she believed. Well, no matter; it was only another vampire myth.

Bianca was already tipsy and playfully fending off her horny boyfriend, Jeremy. She knew they were going to have sex, but she intended to be out on the town for a while first. He never took her anywhere, and she had been thinking lately that she should dump him for a man. Sure, he was a man, but he was very much a boy in the way he behaved. He nuzzled her neck, but just as she was getting into it, she felt a powerful presence on her other side—an intimidating presence. She looked up and found herself staring into the darkest eyes on the most gorgeous face she'd ever seen. Her mouth gaped open as the man gave her a very sexy and inviting smile.

Jeremy looked up when he felt Bianca leaning away from him. He also found himself looking into black, soulless eyes, but they didn't invite him in, they warned him to back down. And instead of a smile, he was met with a smug smirk as the stranger took Bianca's hand and helped her off her stool.

"What the fuck?" Jeremy shouted as his girlfriend walked off with the stranger.

Bianca, lost in a trance, didn't even glance back at her boyfriend, but Devin did—he gave him a glare that was loud and clear. *Let her go—you lose.*

Devin thought taking the woman from her date was too easy, and he wanted to drag it out a little, so he led the starry-eyed woman onto the dance floor. "Take Me Home Tonight" was playing on the jukebox, and he grinned.

I will certainly take you somewhere.

She pressed her body against him as they danced together, and it made him chuckle. He found it amusing that the woman believed she could seduce him—a master of enticement. He was the only predator there.

He asked her in his mesmerizing voice, "What's your name, pretty lady?"

"Bianca," she gasped. She was stunned by how his voice stimulated her. She felt herself swelling between her thighs.

"Good, now I know who I'm going to eat tonight," he replied huskily. She blushed and looked away, assuming, of course, that it was a sexual innuendo.

As soon as the song ended, Devin led her away from the dance floor, the crowd, and the fuming other man. They quietly headed out the door and into the mysterious night. She didn't put up any resistance, not that his female prey ever did.

Not wanting to wait so long to feed his hunger, he took her around the corner of the tavern into the alley. No one was around, not that it mattered much. What could they do to him after all?

Moving slow and sensual, Devin pressed her against the wall and hiked her skimpy skirt with one hand while pressing his other hand against her perky breast. He teased her nipple, which was still hard, but it wasn't as hard as he was. He wasn't surprised Bianca was wearing a thong—her whole outfit screamed *tease*. No wonder her date was so upset. He deftly yanked the panty down and began massaging her nest of downy curls while she tried to kiss him. Wanting her to receive some pleasure before her demise, he moved his finger around her pearly bud while he accepted her tongue into his thirsty mouth. She thrashed her body against his finger as it brought currents of ecstasy to her. This was what she'd been longing for—a man.

"Turn around," he commanded, and she immediately obeyed, thinking his forcefulness was hot.

Much to her delight, the finger that was teasing her before was replaced by his thick, turgid shaft. "Oh God," escaped from her lips as her body stretched around him.

Deeply embedded inside her slick sheath, Devin moved in a rhythmic symphony with her. He kissed the back of her shoulder while pleasuring them both with his long, hard strokes. His fangs ached for her throat, to taste the soft flesh and warm blood. The midnight thirst was upon him, and its call was strong, so his fangs pricked playfully at her exposed shoulder.

Pulsating waves of ecstasy seized Bianca, and her body exploded in sensation down the length of his hardness. Soon after, she was riding yet another wave of exquisite release when she felt a sudden sting in her shoulder. She couldn't focus on it, though, because she was helpless to fight the spasms of rapture pulling her under.

Devin prodded her passion-moistened depths and was flooded with a fountain of molten heat down the length of his shaft. It was amusing to him that he was draining her of bodily fluids at both ends.

They both became aware that someone was watching—it was her date. Devin didn't stop pounding her flesh, though; instead, he continued to thrust—rocking her body and shoving it relentlessly against the wall.

The ripples of ecstasy from her pelvis overrode the feeling of guilt she had over her long-time boyfriend. She met Jeremy's bewildered gaze and felt sorry for him, but she couldn't stop the undulated rapture she was experiencing. She'd try to make it up to him later—so she believed.

Devin took a deep drink from her while he reached his own jarring climax. Her date had run away before seeing her eyes roll back into her head—both from her final glorious peak and from the fatal drop of blood spilled into his ravenous mouth. Her body slumped down the wall and crumpled to the pavement.

Devin decided it was best to deal with the young man as well, and it didn't take him but a mere moment to catch up to the lad and break his neck in one quick movement. The lifeless body collapsed to the ground, and Devin left it there, just as the redhead was still in the alley. Satisfied for now, he shifted into a black cat and slunk back into the night.

Still restless, Devin continued to scour the dark streets for prey. Then something called to him like a siren in the night, and it took him only five blocks to find her. He found a shapely brunette with hair as dark as midnight and a fair complexion that echoed the full moon. She was in a phone booth tapping her foot restlessly while she argued with the person on the other end of the line.

"Because my cell phone died," the vixen said in a tense voice.

In human form, he approached the booth and slid the door open.

"Just a damn minute!" the woman yelled at him without even looking his way.

He quickly reached around her and pressed the hook down.

Salena Saunders spun around, abruptly shouting, "What the hell?"

When her blue eyes met the middle of the man's massive chest, her anger was swallowed and replaced with fear. Slowly, Salena looked up into an extremely attractive face with intense black eyes that frightened her to the core; yet inexplicably, they excited her too.

Devin leaned down and purred into the beautiful woman's ear, "I've been looking for you."

Salena was overcome with panic, but her legs wouldn't move. It wasn't because the massive man filled the small booth, blocking her escape route. It wasn't because he was the most breathtakingly handsome man she'd ever laid her eyes on. It wasn't because he had the most erotic fragrance she'd ever inhaled and the sexiest, most seductive voice she'd ever heard. It was because of the way he looked at her—he wasn't giving her a choice.

His hand clasped her hip, and the heat from his touch seemed to sear her flesh right through her clothing. The contact made her cheeks flush as a scalding heat burned between her thighs.

Devin inhaled and chuckled—he knew he was affecting her. Without delay, he leaned in to tease her perfect full lips; he needed to savor the beautiful creature. Something about her was truly enticing. There was something that set her apart from the others, and he wanted to take his time with the seduction. There was no one around to interrupt him.

As he deepened his kiss and let his hands roam over her form, she began to respond by pressing against him and sucking on his tongue. Yes, he had her spellbound.

Salena tried to stop herself. While her body betrayed her common sense, her mind was wondering what in God's name she thought she was doing making out with a complete stranger in a phone booth. But heaven help her, there was something irresistibly sexy about him. She pressed her breasts into his large, solid chest, and before she could protest, not that she was sure she would have, he ripped her blouse open and began kissing the tops of her soft mounds. A sweltering flame settled in her nipples, and her hands clutched his long hair, urging him to continue. So he did—he tore her bra open as well. Thinking she should care that he was ruining her outfit and that they were in a public area, she hesitated her writhing and looked at him, ready to tell him to stop. His tongue was setting flickers of fire to her rosy tips, and she felt a tiny nip that hurt but also teased—it caused a moan to come from her lips instead of the objection she'd intended. Her body was lusciously tormented by his mouth while his hands hiked her skirt farther up her milky white thighs. She wanted to object, but the words were lost in ragged gasps as flames of passion consumed her. Her thighs moved with a motion of drawing apart and closing together; her body communicated its desire to have a part of him slipping back and forth within her moisture and tightness. He fulfilled her unspoken request by stroking his palm over her concealed mound, using slow circular movements to stoke the flames engulfing her. She felt her intimate parts swell even more and ached for him to deepen his touch. As if he read her thoughts, he blazed a path of kisses down her neck, while forcing the fabric of her panties aside, and he began his circular movements once again—this time on her taut pearl. Her hips lunged forward in response while she clutched at his expansive shoulders. Thoughts of fleeing, again, entered her mind and, again, they were pushed aside by the torment of passion wracking her body.

Devin knew she was conflicted, so he whispered against her neck, "It's futile to resist me."

His tongue flicked over her quickening pulse as her fingernails ground into his solid pecs, urging him on. He used one finger to slip through the softness of her damp petals while his left hand extended her right arm. He wanted just a taste for the time being, so his kisses trailed up her arm to her wrist, which was pinned above her head. He shallowly bit into her wrist, not wanting to spill too much blood just yet. He was too intoxicated with the vixen not to make it last. Something surprising happened, though. As a dribble of her sweet nectar entered his mouth, his mind screamed at him to stop. Something was very wrong about this woman. Completely uncharacteristic of him, he dropped her arm and broke away into the blackness.

Salena, stunned by his rash departure and even more so by her own behavior, pulled her clothing together and hurried to her car before he could return and resume his seduction.

*A*s soon as he reached the cover of trees, Devin turned to watch the vixen flee. He couldn't understand his reaction to her. He never ran away from anything, and he'd certainly never let his prey go free before.

There was still a lingering taste from the small amount of blood he'd taken from her. It was the sweetest, most enticing flavor Devin could recall tasting, and he needed more. Finding her might take time, but it wasn't impossible. Fortunately, the hormones in blood gave each woman a unique flavor, while the pheromones provided a unique scent. His mind went back to her particular scent; she'd smelled like honeysuckle and lavender. Then his thoughts lingered over her beauty—she had porcelain pale skin and black hair that fell past her shoulders and was just as dark as his. He remembered her full red lips and her having the bluest of eyes, too, and a peculiar sense of familiarity caused a chill to run down his spine. He brushed it off and recalled the sweetness of her womanly response to his touch. The memory made his groin grow thick and heavy, and it pressed against its cloth confines—he definitely needed to find the woman and finish what he'd started.

With that thought, he shifted into a black crow and began to scour the city. There were many opportunities to stop for a snack, but this latest creature was his obsession, so he pressed on—he was a starving beast on the hunt. Her black car was impossible to find in the darkness among the other cars on the busy roads, not to mention he didn't know which direction she'd gone. He was confident that he would find her, though. Self-doubt was not in his vocabulary.

Salena woke up late Monday morning with perspiration on her forehead. She'd had an intense dream, but much to her disappointment, it had ended before it really took off. She tried to remember all the sultry details when she noticed a slight stinging in her wrist. Looking down, a wave of panic washed over her—there was a bite mark. It was barely visible, but it was there. It hadn't been just a dream, *just a sex dream,* she thought, and shame flooded her face as she recalled losing all her senses around the mysterious man. She wasn't in the habit of having sex with strangers, especially in public places.

Inhaling deeply, she picked up a faint scent of musk from the torn blouse she still wore. She held the silky material to her nose and breathed in the scent of him. An immediate response emanated from her most sensitive spot and caused her to feel more humiliated. She had never behaved like an utter floozy until that moment in the phone booth.

She wondered what had made him stop and run away. Even more so, she wondered why he'd bitten her. Was that something new in sex? Granted, it had been a while…

Something flickered about the bite in the back of her mind—an article she'd read. She scrambled out of bed and into the kitchen to grab her paper, *The Times-Picayune*, which was lying on the countertop. It didn't take her long to find what she was looking for. A story about a college student who was found dead in her apartment late Saturday night graced the front page. The article stated that the cause of death had not yet been determined, but she had faint markings on her skin which were possibly from an animal bite. Also, evidence of consensual sexual activity was present, so they were looking for a male suspect to question.

Salena turned on the local news to see if there was any additional information on the case, and what she heard sent a tremor of fear running down her spine. Another female victim had been discovered late last night. She also had a bite mark, and again, evidence of consensual sexual activity was present. Additionally, a young male had been found dead with a broken neck not too far from the other crime scene. Authorities were not sure if the recent murders were related, and they currently had no suspects. Police were looking into all three of the recent slayings and trying to find witnesses and a connection between them.

Salena looked at her wrist and felt a wave of nausea overcome her. A thought raced through her mind—she might know who the killer is. She might have almost been his next victim. If he was the killer, though, why did she escape when the others hadn't?

"Wait! I didn't escape, he ran away. But why?" she thought aloud.

She wondered what to do—call the police? How could she describe to the authorities what had happened in the phone booth without lying to them? She couldn't call it attempted rape when she didn't try to fight him off. Hell, she had wanted him to keep going. And what about the other two women? It was classified as consensual sex.

The situation was all so strange, and she didn't do well with strange.

Needing to relax and enjoy what was left of the first day of her vacation from work at The Edgar Degas House, where she worked as a tour guide, Salena decided to work on her oil painting. She hoped it would take her mind off the events of last night and the news. She'd been working on a serene springtime setting. She'd painted flowers, trees, a duck pond with baby ducklings, and a fountain so far. Deciding to finish the duck pond, she engrossed herself in the intricate details of adding a graceful swan treading water when her cell phone rang and startled her. She dropped her brush onto the floor, splattering paint everywhere. In her absentmindedness, she had forgotten to put the drop cloth down first, so now she had a colorful splotch on her plush carpet.

"Shit!" she cursed as she reached for the phone. No name came up on the display, but she recognized the number; she'd called it thousands of times over the course of two years. It was Eric Buchanan—her deepest and last love.

Staring at the phone like she'd never seen one before, she wondered why she'd be hearing from him now, after all this time—two years, three months, and seventeen days to be exact. She answered his call, filled with trepidation. "Hello?"

"Salena?" The sexy deep voice she'd loved so much carried her back to another lifetime. "It's Eric. How are you beautiful?"

"Hi, Eric. I'm fine, but why are you calling?" She caught herself biting her nails while waiting for his response.

"Well, I'm back in town on business, and I hoped to see you tonight for an early dinner or drinks. Do you still live on Canal Street?"

She hesitated to confirm. "Yes, but—"

He cut her off. "No buts. I'll be there in thirty minutes." The phone clicked, and he was gone.

How dare you!

Salena was fuming. It was typical of Eric. He was always calling the shots like when he had proposed to her with a hefty price tag—marry him and move to New York, or...

She had chosen *or*. Her career was as important to her as his was to him. If he'd loved her enough to propose, it should have been enough to stay in the home they'd made together in New Orleans. There were probably still a few of his things buried in her closet—tucked away just like her feelings.

She looked down at her clothes and arms. She was wearing her old paint-stained work clothes and had paint all over her hands and forearms. That'll teach him not to give her any notice.

Eric showed up in exactly thirty minutes, and he was holding a bouquet of her favorite flowers—painted daisies. He looked as handsome as ever, and he'd dressed up to see her. He was in a black suit with a deep blue tie.

With raised eyebrows, she gestured to her casual clothes. "Oh. I obviously wasn't aware that this was a *formal* impromptu dinner or drink thing."

Eric's laughter bounced off the porch beams. "I always did love your sense of humor."

"Who's joking?" she snapped at him. "You didn't give me any notice, and I don't appreciate it."

Eric looked down in shame at his shiny black dress shoes. "Well, it's wonderful to see you, and I'm sorry about the short notice."

"Hello, and you should be. I'm going to go change my outfit." Salena put down her paintbrush and stormed off to her bedroom, shutting the door with more force than she needed to. The nerve of him to put her on the spot like that; she hated it.

The truth was, though, his self-confidence was a quality that had attracted her to him when they'd met almost five years ago, not long after she'd moved to New Orleans. She was at a bistro, enjoying a latte and reading the local paper early one morning, when a forward—albeit gorgeous—man sat down, uninvited, at her table. He'd smiled cockily and told her, "You're new in town. You must be because I'd never overlook such a beautiful woman." Then, before she could respond, he'd handed her a business card and excused himself for a meeting. Insulted, she'd thrown the card in the trash without even looking at it. However, he'd managed to find her again on another occasion and acted like a gentleman that time. She'd surprisingly found him pleasant, and their torrid love affair began.

In the midst of her reverie and changing her clothes, Salena suddenly felt warm hands on her shoulders and hot breath, followed by even hotter kisses, on her neck. Even after two years, he remembered her passion points, and he was hitting every one of them. He turned her around and held her face in one strong hand while the other unfastened her bra.

"I've missed you," he said against her cheek, and then he took her mouth prisoner.

Salena couldn't help but let the man she'd loved with all her heart consume her. She'd missed him too. She hadn't even dated since him. He was hard to measure up to; he was handsome, masculine, intelligent, humorous, confident, and sexy. He was also an amazing lover.

Just as he left her mouth to move down to a cupped breast, she felt her own hands opening his shirt. His torso was as lean and muscled as it had been when he had left, and it still turned her on. She raked her nails down it and circled his nipples while he suckled on hers. She tossed her head back with a low moan.

Should I really be letting him do this? Oh, definitely yes.

Her shorts and pink cotton panties were soon around her ankles, and he slipped a hand between her thighs to stroke her petal-soft folds. His feather-light touches caused her to ache to the very core.

Wasting no time, she helped him remove his suit, and soon, his fully engorged staff sprang free. He picked her up, ravishing her mouth with his plunging tongue, and carried her to the bed. He lay down above her, still kissing her deeply, and then with an arm around her, he rolled over, putting her on top—it was always his favorite position. She eased him into her body, moving down slowly to feel every inch of him grace her slippery softness. In unison, they cried out at the sensation of joining their bodies in splendid rapture. She arched her back and rocked in fluid movement, taking him in as far as he could go. He matched her movements with quick, rigid thrusts that created a shuddering response inside her hot, convulsing center. Screams of pleasure filled the room as their measured, unrelenting rhythm brought them both to their blinding moment of release. Then gasps for air were punctuated with kisses as she fell softly to his side in pure bliss and fell asleep in his embrace.

Salena woke up in a daze. She was still in Eric's embrace, and he was sound asleep yet. She couldn't help but wonder what their lovemaking meant. Was he coming back to her, or expecting her to go back with him? Was it just a booty call while he was in town? She assumed the latter was most likely the case. She quietly got out of bed and grabbed her robe from the closet. After covering her naked body, she headed into the kitchen for some chamomile tea.

With her tea, she stepped outside to sit on her porch swing. She looked at the thermometer she had posted; it read seventy-two degrees, which was typical for that time in May. The muggy air reminded her that rain was in the forecast for the next few days. It was her week on vacation, and she wondered what all she would and should do. For one thing, she needed Eric to get his remaining belongings out of her closet. *Unless he's coming back. No, don't go there.* She felt like a fool for letting herself jump to conclusions.

She slowly swayed back and forth on the swing, thinking about their lovemaking. Hopefully, it would hold her off from attempts at public sex again, she mused to herself. Her behavior with the stranger had been insane. But sex with Eric, well, that was amazing. And to think she had been mad at him for just showing up like that.

She glanced at her lawn, mentally planning a new flowerbed when, suddenly, a black cat jumped over the edge of the porch. Startled, she spilled the hot tea on herself.

"Ouch! Son-of-a-bitch!" Her shout filled the quiet night air and caused the cat to scatter off, which was good because she was about to throw her mug at it.

Eric appeared in the doorframe. "Are you okay?"

"No, I burned myself when a damn cat scared the shit out of me."

Eric couldn't help but laugh at the situation, and his warm laughter eventually drew her in with a giggle of her own. "Where's your first aid kit?"

"I think I have one in the bathroom where we—" she stopped herself and looked down at her bare feet. "Where I've always kept it." She couldn't let herself slip into old habits.

He went back into the house and returned a few minutes later with some burn cream and a cool wet washcloth. She let him tend to the burn on her thigh while running her right hand through his thick blond hair. Then she remembered her wrist and held it under the glow from the porch light. The bite mark was minutely visible. *How can that be?* She wasn't a fast healer, so there had to be another explanation. She hadn't dreamed the whole thing; there was a darker mark there earlier. She shook her head.

"What? You don't like my doctoring skills?" Eric asked with a silly grin.

"Dr. Buchanan, you did a great job," she teased and winked at him. "What do I owe you?"

He scooped her up off the swing and carried her back into the house. "My rates are pretty steep," he said before plundering her mouth once again and then tossing her onto the bed.

Devin had gotten close to her, even though it was only for a second. He didn't mean to scare her and make her burn herself, however, so he felt bad about that. Then as he watched the lovers go inside her house, jealousy filled him. He wanted to be the one to carry her to bed and provide her with endless pleasures. If he ravished her like he wanted to, maybe he could figure out why the woman had a spell over him.

He watched the lovers in action through her bedroom window until he couldn't any longer. Jealousy was new to him, and it left a sour taste in his mouth. There was something about her that haunted him. Something about her was different from other women, and it drew him in. He had to find a way to get close enough to her to find out what it was.

He looked back at the lovers, and hatred replaced his jealousy. He wanted to rip the man in two. He briefly considered breaking into her house and doing just that, but in the end, he decided it wasn't the right time.

He slunk away from her house to search for prey.

Eric left early the next morning. He told her he had a 9:00 flight back to New York, but he would visit her again soon. He grabbed his box of remaining items, which was an uncomfortable exchange Salena had been hoping to avoid indefinitely. It just rubbed salt in the wound. With a last kiss, he headed down her porch steps. *Wham, bam, thank you, ma'am* ran through her mind as she watched him drive away.

She thought she'd tackle a few chores around the house and then go into town. The weather called for sun and mid-eighties temperature, which made for a good day at the farmer's market. She put carpet cleaner on the paint splotch and threw a load of clothes into the washer. When she stepped out onto the porch to grab the morning paper, she was surprised to find a bouquet of wild orchids. She picked them up and looked around, but no one was there. There was no card with the flowers either. She didn't think Eric could've put them there unless he'd circled back, but who else would they be from? She felt cheap again. She put the flowers in water and worked on the carpet stain. Memories of Eric's touch distracted her, though, and brought on a pink flush of arousal while she rubbed at the stubborn stain. She soaked it with stain remover and decided to let it sit for a while. Then she got cleaned up and headed to the French Quarter for some shopping.

The French Quarter was bustling as usual with shoppers, street performers, carriage rides, tour groups, and ladies lunching. Salena overheard a group of women gossiping about the recent murders and looked down at her wrist; it barely had a scratch on it. The way that the bite mark was rapidly disappearing was bone-chilling. She still debated telling the police, but now there was no proof.

Salena looked at the shop signs along the busy sidewalk, wondering where to head next, when a particular sign caught her attention. Unsure of what she was doing, she walked down the block to Marie Laveau's House of Voodoo.

She wasn't sure what she was expecting to find or what she was even looking for—except for answers—but she headed into the shop. She felt overwhelmed by all the paraphernalia: tarot cards, dolls, candles, masks, jewelry, and odds and ends. The items reminded her of her late grandmother's close friend, Heloise Montreuil—a Gypsy woman whose family was into crystal balls, tarot cards, fortune telling, and old-world curses. Throughout Salena's childhood, the colorful woman had often regaled her with stories about white and black magic and seeing the future. She'd even performed a tarot reading for Salena on her thirteenth birthday, which allegedly revealed that she would one day meet a tall, dark, handsome man who would change her destiny. Salena decided to call upon the woman's expertise again, but before she could leave the shop to pay Heloise a visit, a Creole woman stopped her.

"No! You cannot leave yet because I have much to tell you. So, please take a seat and let me help you."

Help me? The question was silent, but the expression on Salena's face wasn't.

The woman spoke with a forceful tone. "You came here for answers, and I have the answers you seek. I saw them in a vision I had last night. It was a vision of a dark stranger who has come into your life unexpectedly, and he brings danger with him. You must search the past to find your answers for the present and your future but beware because not all is what it seems."

Feeling scared and uneasy, Salena tossed a twenty-dollar bill on the counter and left.

Salena met Heloise at the Café Du Monde in the French Quarter. They exchanged a quick hug and kiss on the cheek before sitting down at a secluded table, per Salena's request. She didn't think the other patrons needed to hear what she had to say.

Heloise began with the formality of catching up with her old friend's granddaughter, and Salena followed along until the waiter left with their order for iced teas. Heloise was reminiscing about fun times with Salena's paternal grandmother, Gail, when Salena interrupted her.

"Heloise, I need your advice about something that happened Sunday night, something I can't explain. I was attacked"—she looked down with a blush. It was hard to refer to it as an attack when she had been enjoying herself—"by a man when I was in a phone booth."

Heloise almost choked on her sip of tea. "Oh my! Are you all right, dear? Did you report it to the police?"

Salena blushed again and decided to leave out the intimate parts. "I'm okay. Nothing really happened except for this." She flipped over her wrist, so Heloise could examine the bite mark, but it was even less visible than earlier.

Heloise peered closely at Salena's wrist, "I'm not sure what I'm supposed to be looking at."

Salena felt like a fool. She cleared her throat and softly stated, "He bit me."

The older woman's face paled. "He bit you on the wrist?"

Salena simply nodded in response, and Heloise placed a wrinkled hand over her heart.

"The women in the news had bite marks on them. You're lucky to be alive, Salena," she quietly announced.

Salena nodded. "I know I am. I wonder if it is the same man, though." *And you wouldn't believe what I almost did with him.*

"Let me see your wrist again."

She held out her wrist, feeling like such an idiot about the entire experience.

"I don't see a bite mark, though." Heloise peered at the young woman over her reading glasses.

"He kissed me first, and then he bit me," she quietly replied.

"Something is odd about these attacks. Let's go to my house and consult the tarot cards," the Gypsy offered.

Salena laid money on the table for the drinks and followed Heloise the four miles to her cottage. Neither woman noticed the black wolf following them along the tree line.

Devin kept pace with the women—he'd been watching and following Salena all day. It had taken some time to locate her, but he'd finally found her scent when he was a black hawk and flew over the French Quarter. She had been walking out of a voodoo shop, with a look of deep concern on her beautiful face, when he'd caught her scent. It was her unmistakable alluring fragrance of honeysuckle and lavender.

At the café, he'd heard the older woman address her as Salena, and he thought it was a beautiful name. He'd noticed the talisman the old woman wore and figured she must be a Gypsy. He'd overheard their entire conversation, and it piqued his interest. When they stopped at the Gypsy's cottage, he shifted back into a cat and perched on the windowsill to listen attentively. He wanted insight into the situation as well.

As soon as the front door closed, Heloise bustled into the other room to get her deck of tarot cards. Then she spread them out on the coffee table and told Salena to choose three. Salena did as she was instructed; although, she was still not sure what she expected to accomplish. She was desperately looking for answers, however, regardless if they were logical or not.

"The first card represents the past," Heloise said and flipped the card over. "Death."

Salena gasped at the word.

"Don't worry, dear. It's not necessarily about you or anyone dying. Let's see what the second card is before we determine the meaning of the first." Heloise flipped the second card. "Fool," she said, looking back at the first. "Hmm…let's see the last card." Her withered hand flipped over the final card. "Tower." She looked at all three cards and then at Salena's concerned and curious face. "You must come to terms with something from the past because it is in your present. Not everything is what it seems to be, and in the future, you are going to find out that some of your core beliefs are false. Salena, you will have to open up your mind to accept what was, what is now, and what is destined to come. I see danger in your life now, and it has something to do with the past. We must look at what happened long ago." With that, she got up and headed into another room of the small house.

Salena sat there, feeling bewildered and thinking about the woman from the voodoo shop and her "vision." The tarot reading, not that she believed in such things, sounded very similar.

So, what does that mean?

Heloise returned to the living room with a dusty old book in her hands and a look of apprehension on her wrinkled but wise face. "This is a diary that belonged to my great-great-great-great-great grandmother who died right here in Louisiana in 1724. I can remember, from my young adult years, reading about some horrifying events during my grandmother's life in the colony. I'm afraid that if I'm right, the devil himself has come back, and he has set his sights on you."

Shocked, Salena jumped up from the sofa and paced the small room, trying to assess what that could mean. Heloise was thumbing through the book, and Salena was surprised by how fast the old woman's fingers could move. Salena glanced at the pages when Heloise paused, but she couldn't make out any of the words because the book was written in French. She studied the Gypsy's face as she flipped the crinkled yellowed pages, and then she saw a look of recognition in Heloise's timeworn eyes.

The woman clutched the talisman she wore with one hand and took Salena's wrist in the other to look at the faded bite mark again. She looked into the young woman's anxious eyes while wringing her wrinkled hands nervously.

"Could it be?" she whispered with wide eyes.

"Could it be what? What did you read?" Salena yelped and stood frozen in place.

Heloise turned another page in the book. "I think you've been chosen," she said in a foreboding tone.

Salena started pacing again, feeling restless, and threw her hands up. "Chosen for what?" Her voice came out tense and shrill, and she started to bite her nails. It was an old nervous habit, and with her current stressors, she'd never grow them out again.

Heloise turned more pages. "Her diary speaks of a dark and handsome stranger who was in the colony at the same time that several young women were left seduced and lifeless. Faint markings that resembled bite marks were found on the bodies. It was the only proof that he'd been there. The proof mysteriously vanished, though, by the time the bodies were burned. The colonists thought it must be a plague because they didn't know what had caused the young, healthy women to suddenly die and turn ashen. That was their reason for burning the bodies.

"My grandmother wrote that only the Gypsies suspected otherwise, and there was one woman who was bitten but mysteriously survived. She was a young widow with an infant son. My grandmother wrote that she was 'strikingly beautiful with milky white skin, raven-black hair, and eyes the color of a clear sky.'"

Heloise stopped and looked at Salena. "She sounds a lot like you." Salena looked down at her wrist, and Heloise glanced in its direction also.

"The visitor had been seen with her often, leaving more bite marks on her neck and wrist, yet her life had still been spared, and the marks seemed to disappear right before their eyes. She had tried to conceal them, but they were discovered, nonetheless, and the colonists accused her of being the devil's mistress—a witch—and they burned her alive in her home. After that, the devil disappeared. Her son had escaped with a servant and was raised by his uncle in another colony."

Heloise turned the page, and then her face showed comprehension. She looked at Salena with an expression of foreboding. "The condemned woman's name was Abigail Saunders."

Salena plopped down hard on the sofa, shaken to the core by that piece of information. Her full given name was Salena Abigail Saunders—after a long distant grandmother, according to her late father.

"It says here," Heloise continued with angst in her voice, "the Gypsies thought he was a vampire, and I think he might have returned." She tapped the newspaper on the table by the tarot cards; the front-page story was about the female victims. Then she put her hand on Salena's wrist. "You must be careful, girl. This isn't a New Orleans tourist attraction—your life really is in great danger."

In a daze, Salena hurriedly left Heloise's house and drove home. *A vampire is after me? Get real. There's no such thing.*

She decided that the first thing she needed to do was search for her family tree that she'd come across years ago. When her parents had died in an accident, she'd found it in their belongings. Having no siblings, she took that and the other mementos with her when she moved from the family's estate in Philadelphia to New Orleans. Her remaining relatives had thought she was crazy to move so far away, and maybe they were right, but at that time, she'd needed to get away from the pain of her loss. She knew her MA in History Degree would help her find work in any museum wherever she decided to go; however, something pulled her to New Orleans. She used to think it was Eric.

She spread the yellowed document out on her kitchen table and used her index finger to run up the line through her father's relatives. There it was—Abigail Saunders, born nee Abigail Adams in 1696, died in 1720.

Salena was even more morose to learn her great-grandmother to the tenth generation was only twenty-four when she'd died. Salena had just turned twenty-four two months ago. The disconcerting information brought fearful tears to her blue eyes—the blue eyes she'd inherited, along with her porcelain skin and black hair. She had teased her parents several times about being adopted because her mother had been a redhead with green eyes, while her father had sported brown hair and brown eyes. It was suddenly clear where her traits had come from, and a chill coursed through her, causing her to violently shiver.

She'd never heard the story that her great-grandmother had been accused of witchcraft and had been killed for it. She thought about the history of witch trials and could remember certain events in colonial history regarding them, but she certainly couldn't remember anything about *vampires*. She had to get to the bottom of things, and time was of the essence.

She stepped out onto her small porch and sat on the swing; she always sat there to clear her head. Her tearful eyes searched her yard and then her neighbors' yards— every corner, every shrub, every shadow—making sure nothing was there. *Is my life really in danger?* The words screamed in her mind. She had thought living alone in a largely populated city was dangerous enough. *Now I have a fictional monster to fear? Do vampires exist outside the tours and haunted cemeteries?* She couldn't wrap her head around that even as she fingered where the bite mark had been on her wrist. *Had been...*It was completely gone now.

She needed more information, so she headed back inside to go through her history books. She never noticed the black cat sitting behind her.

Devin had followed Salena back to her home, contemplating what he'd seen at the Gypsy's house. Unfortunately, he wasn't able to overhear much of their conversation because a radio had been playing loudly in the background. He knew Salena was upset, and he'd overheard something about "danger from the past." However, he hadn't heard enough to know what that meant, and he'd never learned how to read tarot cards; Gypsies and vampires weren't exactly friends.

His questions remained unanswered, so at her home, he'd watched from his perch on her windowsill while she'd recovered something scrolled up in a drawer that appeared to be a family tree.

He loved how graceful she was when she moved through her house, and the sound of her voice was exquisite—it was soft and delicate like the sound of a gentle rain hitting flower petals. Her hair reminded him of a raven's wings as it flowed in the breeze behind her along with the breathtaking fragrance of honeysuckle and lavender.

Then she'd come outside and sat on her porch swing. He'd gotten close to her, sitting behind her, and wondered if he should shapeshift back into himself and approach her; however, something stopped him—and he still didn't know what. Then, just a few minutes later, she got up and went back into her house.

He watched her again through her windows while she paced the floors of her home. She was searching for something in the drawers and bookcases. Then he saw relief flood her face as she held a thick book.

Salena studied one of her old history texts on colonial times. She read and reread about the witch trials and accusations, but she didn't see anything about Abigail Saunders or vampires—not even in the section that mentioned the Gypsies.

Staring blankly at the wall, she almost jumped out of her skin when her cell phone rang. The caller ID revealed that it was Michael Payne. *Great.* She had second thoughts about picking up. He had been asking her out for months, but she was hesitant to date him. He was boring, plain, and better suited as a friend; she just couldn't imagine having butterflies or sparks with him. Not after Eric.

She'd met Michael six months ago at work, when the historical home hired him as a security guard; although, she couldn't imagine any aspiring criminal feeling threatened by him. He was a short man, and the way he carried himself didn't portray confidence. He rarely made eye contact with people, Salena included, and he spoke in a quiet voice. All were reasons why Salena couldn't see herself being romantically involved with him—he just wasn't masculine. If she were to start dating again, it would have to be with a handsome, virile, sexy, and strong man—

like Eric. However, she hadn't been looking for love lately; she was still too hurt.

The reason for Michael's call was to invite her to dinner at her favorite Italian restaurant, Vincent's Italian Cuisine. Thinking that a quiet dinner in a public place might calm her nerves, she finally accepted. Her condition, though, was that it was "only as friends and Dutch treat."

After an hour of thumbing through her books, Salena hopped into the shower, feeling foolish as she locked the bathroom door and double-checked the window lock. She lived alone in a safe neighborhood and had never felt the need to be overly cautious...until now. *According to legends, vampires—assuming they really do exist—cannot go out into daylight anyway, right?* Then again, it was supposed to be just a legend, so if it wasn't, who knew what the rules really were.

An hour later, she headed out the door to meet Michael at the restaurant. She'd told him she'd drive herself, thinking that letting him pick her up would feel too much like a date.

She had no idea that every move she made was being watched and studied. Every inch of her body had also been studied while she was in the shower.

Watching her made Devin grow hot and heavy with lust. He ached to touch all that he saw—soon.

Michael was already waiting for her when she arrived at Vincent's. Being a gentleman, he held the door open for her and the other ladies close behind, and he pulled her chair out for her too.

Devin watched the scrawny man's behavior with amusement. The fool was trying hard to impress Salena, but she didn't seem to care.

Devin was back in human form and found a dark corner near their table to keep an eye on the mysterious vixen. Just as he sat down, a lustful blond and her two female companions approached him. He gave the women a cold, dark glare that quickly sent them away. He only hungered for Salena; although, that fact continued to puzzle him. He supposed it was because he always got what he wanted—except for the other night when he'd fled.

He watched Salena and her date talk quietly through their meal and wondered why she didn't smile much when the man couldn't seem to stop. Devin wondered if she was thinking of him, of their passionate encounter.

He overheard the man ask her how she was enjoying her vacation. She simply replied, "It's been eventful."

Devin was satisfied to see that the date, if it was a date, didn't last too long. He slipped into line behind them when they were on the way out. Salena stopped suddenly and glanced over her left shoulder, but he dodged right and off to her date's side before she could spot him. It was exciting to know that she could feel his presence.

Salena felt the hairs stand up on the back of her neck, and a chill ran down her spine. However, when she looked over her shoulder, no one was there. She was sure she was being watched, though. But, of course, she would be jumpy after the other night and her meeting with Heloise, so she tried to push it from her mind.

There was a pleasant gentle breeze out, and all the stars were lit up. She inhaled deeply, catching the sweet fragrance of the magnolia trees lining the street, but then there was something else—something musky and familiar. Again, she looked around in panic, but again, she didn't see the man she thought she'd find. Not wanting to cross his path again, if he was indeed the killer being sought, she said a very quick goodnight to Michael and hurried to her car parked nearby. She also hurried away because she was sure Michael was hoping for a goodnight kiss.

An hour later, Salena climbed into bed. She was grateful to be on vacation because she'd hate to be distracted at work by what was going on. With her eyes searching the dark room, she ran through mental images of her house, thinking of every lock and assuring herself it had been checked. That wasn't enough, though, so she got back up and checked every one of them again.

While in the living room, she turned on the late news and soon regretted it. The coverage was about the three unsolved murders. Autopsies, so far, only showed that the female victims had died of exsanguination, but the ME wasn't sure how since the only wounds were the small—and strangely fading—bite marks. The newscaster distastefully joked that maybe they had been attacked by a vampire, which made his colleague gape, and Salena about fell out of her chair. Feeling overwhelmed with stress, she turned the TV off and sat on the floor to perform yoga stretches. After the relaxing moves, she decided to paint to further calm her. Every stroke of the brush to complete the tranquil scene on the canvas helped soothe her frayed nerves, and eventually, she was ready to go back to bed. Thinking of only pleasant things, she inescapably drifted off to sleep.

Devin watched the steady rise and fall of her chest as she slept. She looked peaceful as the moonlight streamed across her delicate features. He wondered what she was dreaming about and then wondered why he cared; he'd never cared before. This woman was only supposed to be his next meal; however, there was a magnetic pull to her, and he had to find out why. He didn't want to harm her, he just wanted to be close to her. He desperately wanted to taste her again. The last thought made him creep closer to her bed.

He could smell the honeysuckle and lavender again, and he could also smell her pheromones calling out to him like a siren to a ship—enticing him to come closer, to take a taste. He knelt beside her bed and kissed her bared shoulder where her nightgown had slipped away. She only stirred briefly, so he continued a trail across her collarbone to her slender neck. Nuzzling her sensitive area caused her to wake, but he spoke to her in a hypnotic and sensual voice. He spoke in his old language—Romanian. "Visezi doar. Relaxează-te pentru mine." *You're just dreaming. Relax for me.*

Salena wasn't quite so sure she was dreaming, but she felt like she couldn't move, couldn't voice her objections. She was overwhelmed by the erotic feel of his lips on her neck and the virile musk filling her nostrils. She knew she was in danger, but lust overtook her senses as his hand began to roam over her nightgown, touching lightly at first and then firmly as it moved up her hip. His other hand was caressing strands of her hair as his mouth moved over the length of her neck and trailed its way to her mouth. When he claimed her lips, fear escaped bit by bit, and passion took hold. Instead of pushing him away, she found herself clutching his shoulder in one hand and his massive bicep in the other, pulling him toward herself.

God, what is wrong with me? she silently scolded herself, but her body didn't listen.

His firm tongue thrust in and out of her demanding mouth, teasing, taunting, and causing her body to wriggle. She matched his moves by sucking on his tongue gently, which brought out a low growl from his throat.

She couldn't help but notice how sharp his teeth felt when she grazed one with her tongue.

She felt his hand slide up her waist to cup her breast, kneading the tissue and tormenting her puckered bud. He was expertly working her into a heated frenzy…all over again. *Again?*

She hesitated and looked at him in the moonlight that was barely peeking through her window. Large, sexy, musky—yes, it was him again. She had to be dreaming. There was no other explanation for him to show up in her home and bed. Feeling like she could really let go in her dream, she claimed his lips and pushed his hand off her breast and down her body.

Devin knew he had her under his spell, and he let her guide his fingers to her satiny depths. She groaned with desire as he teased her mound with light touches before moving to the opening of her hot sheath. She dug her claws into his chest, urging him to plunder her moistness, but he answered her groans with a fervent whisper against her neck.

"Not too much tonight, my beauty. You only get a taste."

Suddenly, she felt a piercing sting that made her cry out.

Devin sipped from the puncture mark, lapping up the sweet—so sweet—taste of her essence. He briefly wondered if he could stop, and it wasn't because he was all that hungry. It was because she tasted like nothing he'd had in...He tried to remember how many years, but he couldn't. There was something so uniquely warm, fulfilling, enticing, and almost sinful about her flavor. He thought he had died and gone to heaven. Then, as a glow filled his body, there was something recognizable about her wonderful flavor after all.

Devin looked into Salena's hazy, lustful, crystal-blue eyes and immediately felt a terrifying pang in his chest. Her taste, her features, his obsession...It came back to him on a tidal wave of pain—Abigail. Distressed by the realization and the only painful memory he possessed, he fled from her arms, her bed, and her home—out into the night.

The loud, heartrending howl of a mystified wolf didn't even faze Salena as she drifted off into a deep slumber.

Under the cover of darkness behind Salena's house, Devin's mind was racing, trying to figure the mystery out—the connection between her and Abigail, the only woman he'd ever cared about. No, that wasn't strong enough of a description for her. Abigail was the only woman who had been able to remind him he had a beating heart once, because he had felt it beat again when he had been in her captivating presence. When she had been taken from him—before her love could turn him mortal again—he had sworn he would never let himself feel anything for a woman ever again. He was a vampire, not a mortal, for a reason. He wasn't meant to love. Being damned to walk the earth for all eternity was better than the suffering he had felt when Abigail had died. He would just take what he wanted and never give of himself again.

How can this be? What kind of magic is this? He wished he knew what the Gypsy had told her. *Is she a ghost? Is she a witch trying to torment me?* He needed answers, and he needed them immediately.

He was still outside her house, watching and waiting. He shifted into a black cat again when the sun started to come up over the treetops. Soon, he heard her alarm clock beeping from inside the house, and he knew he'd get to see her again. While that excited him, it also made him anxious. He had to find out more. What was her connection to Abigail? He had to get a look inside her house and learn more about her. He'd start by looking at the family tree and books she'd been examining.

Is that why she was looking at them? Does she know something? Are they books of magic spells? His cat fangs were grinding from the tension he felt.

The alarm clock went off, sending Salena bolting upright in bed. Feeling groggy from a restless sleep, she began to remember her lustful dream. Even in the morning light, it had her aroused. She had dreamed about her mystery man from the phone booth. She remembered his long, drugging kisses with perfect clarity. She also remembered the feel of his warm, strong hands as they roamed all over her body, stoking flames of desire within her. She could still feel the ache between her creamy white thighs from his teasing touches there. But that was when the dream had ended. Just like in the phone booth, he'd worked her body into frenzy and then abruptly left her. Was the man the Kissing Bandit or what? It would figure that even her dreams would leave her feeling frustrated and unfulfilled.

A dull sting in her neck brought her back to the present, though, and with eyes wide open, she ran to the bathroom mirror. There it was—a telltale mark that said last night wasn't a dream. It couldn't have been—there was a bite mark very similar to the one that had been on her wrist, which had now completely faded away. She wondered if she was losing her mind and seeing things, or if somehow, he'd found her and gotten into her home. As she fingered the slightly painful puncture wounds, she knew she was definitely not imagining it. She felt a flood of panic wash over her body, but it quickly gave way to another feeling—curiosity. Why did the man come to her twice now and then leave her all of a sudden with both her life and virtue intact? She wondered if the latter bothered her more than it should. He had spent the time, twice now, working her body into a molten pool of desire but didn't follow through. Even as she stared in the mirror, instead of calling the police and then running for her life like she should be, she was undeniably lascivious. She was lusting the stranger, the sexy man, the killer of women—except her. *What in God's name is wrong with me? Am I crazy or just a masochist?*

She fingered the bite mark again. What was the biting all about? Then her thoughts returned to her conversation with Heloise and to her tenth-generation great-grandmother, who had also been bitten by a mysterious man. She'd have to speak to Heloise again before he returned to her. Would he return to her? She felt certain of it. This brought back the other concern—how did he get into her house? Everything had been locked up tight, so was there no way to keep him out? And why didn't she try to fight him off either time? She answered her own questions in one word—*vampire.*

What could she tell the police? Would she tell them that a killer got into her locked up home, seduced her, and bit her before running away, and by the way, she thinks he's a vampire? That would go over really well, and she'd be the one locked up—in the nuthouse. Yes, she had to see Heloise after her trip to the farmer's market.

After inspecting all the window and door locks, which were still secured, she took a steamy shower and got ready for her errands. While putting on her makeup, she grabbed her concealer to cover the bite mark, but surprisingly, it wasn't as visible. Was it fading? She glanced again at her flawless wrist where the other mark had been as of yesterday, and she recalled the comments made in Heloise's grandmother's diary. She decided seeing the Gypsy couldn't wait, so she put off shopping until afterward.

It was a dreary day, and when she stepped out the front door, she didn't even notice the black cat that walked past her and around to the back of her house.

On the way to Heloise's, Salena called her cell phone and learned she wasn't home, so her visit would have to wait. Heloise told her not to worry; they would do another reading soon.

Feeling the need for the company of friends, though, Salena called up some girlfriends and invited them to dinner. Then, needing to stock her refrigerator, she headed in the direction of the farmer's market.

Once inside the cover of her living room, where the curtains were closed, Devin shifted back. He had to learn as much as he could about the woman before he visited her again, and he would definitely be visiting her again, no matter who or what she was.

He looked around her pristine home, admiring her choice of knick knacks and décor. Then he went to the drawer where he'd seen her put the family tree back. He took it to her kitchen table, flattened it out, and quickly found her name at the bottom—Salena Saunders. *Saunders...* Alarmed, he hastily ran his finger up Salena's bloodline. There it was—Abigail Saunders.

"They are blood relatives," he whispered to the empty room. "I can't believe it."

He stared at the parchment in absolute astonishment. His truelove's blood flowed through Salena's body, and he'd tasted it. For the first time in almost three hundred years, he saw his destiny again. She didn't know it yet, but Salena was his reincarnated soulmate, his savior. It was meant to be. Abigail had found her way back to him.

He walked through Salena's small and quaint house, taking in the scent of her with flared nostrils. He smelled not only her perfume but also her essence—the pheromones that made her a desirable woman—and he couldn't get enough. The scent made his fangs ache and his pulsing manhood as well. He longed to hold her close, breathing in her fragrance to the fullest, before sinking his teeth in to taste her again. Those thoughts made him hungry beyond comprehension, and he needed to feed. But first, he needed to find her again. He needed to lay his eyes on his destiny, which was clear to him once more.

He headed in the same direction he'd seen her go earlier. Shifted into a black hawk, it wouldn't take him long to find her, he thought, and he was right.

Salena was walking through the farmer's market, picking out some fresh vegetables for a garden salad, when she felt something against her leg. Looking down, she discovered a black cat rubbing up against her.

"Go away," she said and gave the animal a light pat on its hindquarters.

She liked cats, but allergies kept her from having one. The stray cat moved away, but before she knew it, it was back and rubbing again. It purred so loudly that she could feel the vibrations on her leg. She shrugged and returned to her shopping.

A rumble of thunder caught her attention. She looked up at the sky and saw thunderstorm clouds rapidly rolling in. She paid the vendor for her vegetables and quickly moved on down the line, only pausing when a rain breeze carrying a familiar musky scent blew past her. Looking around herself, she didn't see him—or at least whom she thought he was—lurking nearby. Brushing it off, she and the attached cat stopped at a flower vendor. She was looking at a bouquet of painted daisies when the first raindrops fell. Just as she was digging for her wallet, the downpour began, and she ran away, abandoning both the flowers and the cat.

Safely inside a clothing shop, she watched the other market patrons making their mad dashes for cover while the vendors were desperately trying to protect their wares. Since it appeared she would be in the store for a while, she decided to look at the clothes. She shifted the wet bag of vegetables in her arms, so they wouldn't rip through the damp paper. A kind sales clerk offered to keep the bag behind the counter, so she could look at the clothing racks, and she gratefully accepted. She looked through the new merchandise, filled with bright spring and summer colors, and picked out a few new blouses and skirts for work. "Retail therapy," a phrase her mother had often used, came to mind and made her smile. She wondered with a heavy heart what her parents would think about the current events in her life. They were always strict about who they'd let her date when she was growing up, so she was pretty certain they would disapprove of a vampire being in her life, even if her great-grandmother had one first.

After paying for her clothes, she waited out the rain with several others.

Devin was still tingling from the close contact of rubbing up against Salena, even though he'd been a cat at the time. He was back in human form and on the way to her house with the flowers she'd been admiring. He'd grabbed them when the vendor had closed everything up and ran for cover from the rain. Along the way, he noticed a young woman, who was probably in her late teens, standing alone on the sidewalk in front of a dilapidated store. Her white lacy top was drenched and transparent enough to show that she wasn't wearing a bra. Rosy buds peeked through at him, begging to be touched by a man. She shifted her hips and crooked her finger with a seductive smile, but he just laughed silently to himself. It was always amusing when females thought they were the charmers when it came to him. He was the alpha—every time. Nonetheless, he was hungry for blood, so he played along. He approached her with a smile and looked her up and down.

"Good afternoon. Are you trying to stay dry?" he murmured.

She cocked her head and tried to make her voice sultry. "I'm *all* wet. Come inside here with me," she offered while gesturing to the dilapidated building.

The door opened without any resistance, apart from the loud moan of its rusted hinges, and he followed her into the abandoned store. He looked around the rundown building.

"What is this place?" he asked.

She, too, looked around. "I'm not sure, but I think it was a grocery store or something. Right now, though, it can be a place to get to know *you* better." She turned and looked at the flowers in his hand, batting her lashes at him playfully. "Are those for me?"

"No," he grumbled, and as she approached him with a seductive sway of her hips, he added, "I don't have time for this." He sank his fangs into her throat and had his dinner.

Satiated for the time being, he left her body there with the rats and headed back to Salena's house to leave her the flowers. She wasn't home yet, so he left them by her garden tub and looked around some more. He became especially interested in her painting, and being artistic himself, he added a few brush strokes where she had hesitated on the fountain.

When he heard her car in the driveway, he went down through the basement door and left the same way he'd come in.

Still drenched from the rain, Salena pulled into her driveway. A hot bubble bath was definitely in order. She needed to get ready for her dinner plans anyway. After putting her vegetables in the refrigerator, she put her wet clothes into the washing machine and put her new ones in the hamper. She suddenly stopped and turned around— she was sure she could smell the musky fragrance again. She sniffed the air and scowled. Shaking her head, she padded off toward the bathroom for a long relaxing soak.

I'm just imagining things. Or maybe I'm not. She was sure she could smell the enticing musky fragrance throughout her house. But she already knew he'd been there last night, so the scent had to be lingering. The memory of their encounter made her check all the locks again.

Confident that they were secure, Salena headed back down the hallway toward the bathroom. She stopped in the doorway, though, because a vase full of painted daisies—the same daisies she'd eyed earlier—was on the ledge of her tub. She ran back into the kitchen, and sitting on the kitchen counter, was the vase full of flowers from Eric. Someone had gotten inside the house again.

He's been inside my house again. Is he still here? Terrified, she ran to her bedroom and locked the door. *Would that even do any good?* She quickly threw on clothes and called the police.

About thirty panic-filled minutes later, Officer Ann Marx showed up and looked around. She investigated all the doors and windows and saw for herself that nothing had been tampered with. She did notice that the basement door didn't have a lock, though, so she cautioned Salena about that. Then she went downstairs and checked it out. All she saw was the locked patio door with a small built-in pet door. All the windows were intact and locked.

"And you're sure you didn't buy the flowers for yourself?" She had her head tilted with a skeptical look on her face.

Salena cleared her throat. "No. I mean, yes, I'm sure I didn't buy them. The storm started in before I had the chance, and I'm not that forgetful," she explained. *I'm just crazy is all, and I have a vampire after me,* she added on a side note to herself.

The officer looked at her and shrugged. "Well, the crime scene techs have dusted for prints, so we'll see what turns up."

Before she could leave, Salena stopped her. "Wait! There's this too." She pulled her collar aside to expose her neck to the officer.

"What are you trying to show me? I don't see anything," the police officer told her with knitted brows.

Salena ran to the bathroom mirror and looked for herself; it was gone—completely. Officer Marx looked at her with deep concern.

"I think you should lie down and get some rest. Is there someone we can call for you?"

Salena thought about it and suddenly remembered her plans. "No, that's fine. I'll be going to dinner with my friends shortly."

"Good. Don't forget to install a lock on your basement door, and always call if you suspect a break-in," the officer told her. As she was climbing into her car, Salena saw her shake her head.

"Yep, she thinks I'm loco," Salena said aloud as she watched the police leave. Then she called her friends to say she'd be a little late for dinner.

After triple checking the locks, she got ready for her night out with the girls. She hadn't noticed the black cat watching her through the window the entire time.

A shadow played across the building, so Shannon walked faster to her car, ankles wobbling, wishing she hadn't worn her damned spiked heels. It had been a big waste anyway. She was tired of going to bars in the hopes of finding "Mr. Right." At the moment, feeling terrified about the idea of being followed to her car in the pitch-blackness, she especially wished she'd stayed home alone.

As she fumbled in her clutch for her keys, her car parked only a few feet away, she was sure she could hear footsteps closing in behind her. Her hands trembled while she tried to get the key in the lock.

Please, God, don't let me be found dead here in this parking lot ran through her mind just as a large hand covered her mouth, and a sharp pain pierced her neck. As she felt her warm blood—and life—spilling out, she knew her worst fear was coming true.

The woman in the parking lot was not to his taste, but she was enough to hold him over for the moment. She had smelled of cigarettes and booze instead of the French perfumes he preferred, but prey was prey, and it had come time for him to return to the United States for a family reunion. Gabriel knew it was time to find his long-lost brother, Devin.

24

Devin followed Salena back into town. Standing outside a seafood restaurant, he watched her talk animatedly to her friends. He could tell by their posture and gestures that they were close. While the other two women were also lovely, they paled in comparison to Salena. Still, if he had not found his mate, he would've slaked his lust with both of them, before feasting on their blood.

The women proceeded to the maître d' to claim their reservation. He, too, looked them all over in admiration before passing them off to an attractive waiter, whose eyes were instantly fixed on Salena. Devin felt his muscles tense when the waiter made a brash move by putting his palm on the small of Salena's back as he led the women to their table. Devin had no patience to wait in the long line, nor did he intend to let the waiter step any further into his territory. His animal instincts were running strong, and he wanted to tear the man limb from limb—in fact, he likely would. Devin approached the maître d', pushing past angry customers and meeting their questioning stares and comments with a glare that would make a giant back down. The maître d' and a waitress, who was standing near the door, both shuffled aside to let him pass. Devin caught the waitress's scent and added her to the menu for later.

Inside the dimly lit restaurant, he found Salena and her two companions seated at a table, browsing their menus. He also found, almost to his twisted pleasure, the horny waiter hovering nearby Salena. A low, menacing growl escaped his lips, causing a nearby patron to jump from surprise and quickly dart away. A different waiter approached him with a menu, but Devin's fierce glare made him think twice, and he moved on as well. Keeping his stare on Salena and the annoying waiter at her elbow, Devin moved to an out of the way spot in a darkened corner to keep watch. It set his fangs on edge when the waiter leaned in to whisper something in her ear and caused her to erupt into a peel of laughter. Having eyesight sharper than an eagle's, Devin zeroed in on the waiter's nametag, which read *Chad*.

Devin spoke in a whisper, "Well, Chad, soak up the sight of her while you still can. I promise it won't be much longer." No one heard him, of course, but the waiter did turn around to look behind himself.

Devin's attention went back to Salena and her blond friend, who was talking rapidly and passing around a photograph for Salena and the other woman to look at. He used his vampire eyesight and hearing to catch their conversation, which unnerved him as much as the waiter.

The blond was excited when she turned to Salena and said, "You have to meet Rob. I've told him all about you, and he really, really wants to take you out. Look how cute he is."

Salena looked at the photo and shrugged. "Maybe."

The redhead, who had been checking out the flirtatious waiter, wolf whistled. "Chad appears awfully eager to be in line to date you as well." Salena blushed at the obvious statement, and her blond friend broke out in laughter.

The blond, whom he heard Salena refer to as Jane, got up from her seat, grabbed her purse, and told the other women she had to go out to her car to retrieve Rob's phone number from her briefcase.

Salena blushed again and mumbled, "All right."

Devin trailed the unsuspecting Jane out to her car. She didn't even bother to check over her shoulder, which labeled her an easy victim for all predators. She was at her car before she noticed his presence behind her. Her faced turned ghostly pale as he got closer.

She looked around for help, any kind of help, but the lot was empty. "What do you want?" she squawked.

He got close to her and brushed his hand against her pretty cheek and into her hair, not saying anything in response. She was staring up at him, and the look in her eyes changed from total terror to something else—desire. He knew what she was expecting and wanting him to do to her, and under other circumstances, he might have obliged.

He leaned in close as if to kiss her and whispered, "I want you to stop trying to come between Salena and me."

Jane had no idea what he was talking about. "Salena? I don't understand."

The passionate look on her face was once again a look of horror as his seductive touch turned firm. Then she felt the life being squeezed out of her as his right hand closed around her neck. Her pleading eyes bulged, and her mouth gaped open while useless hands clawed at him, and then her fragile neck snapped. It was over. Devin put the lifeless body into the driver's seat and reached over it to grab the briefcase from the passenger's seat. He rifled through it until he found a scrap of paper with *Rob 282— 555—5155* written on it. He tossed the briefcase back into the seat and slipped the number into his pocket.

He didn't drink from her because that's not what killing her was about. He felt regret, which was unheard of for a vampire, but he didn't like hurting Salena. He felt he had no choice in the matter, though. He wouldn't tolerate interference in his plans for his mate.

26

As Devin was walking back to the restaurant, he noticed Salena's waiter, Chad, standing off to the side of the building, smoking a cigarette. He smiled broadly; this was the perfect time to take care of that matter.

Chad saw Devin approaching him with clenched fists and a look of pure malice on his face. Trying to appear tougher than he felt at the moment, he dropped the cigarette, snuffing it out with the toe of his sneaker, and snapped, "What the hell do you want? I'm on my break."

Devin could have made it quick, but he didn't want to, he wanted to watch the man suffer—suffer as his heart did when Salena had smiled back at the waiter with a look of interest in her eyes. Chad would definitely suffer for having lustful thoughts about another's mate—*a vampire's mate.*

Not wanting to cause a disturbance right outside the restaurant—in case Salena came looking for her friend—Devin punched Chad in his smug looking face hard enough to knock him out. In fact, he even heard the unmistakable sound of bone breaking. *Good.* He grinned with wicked pride. He easily threw the man over his thick shoulder and carried him off into the night.

Devin found a vacant campsite that would work well for his plans. The full moon was shining down brightly, which was perfect—he wanted to see the expression of terror on the punk's face when he realized what was happening. He also wanted his own image to be burned into Chad's brain in case there was an afterlife. He just had to wait for Sleeping Beauty to wake up, and that was fine because he had all the time in the world.

Jane hadn't returned from her car yet, and it had been at least fifteen minutes, so Salena was worried about her. Karen had already checked the ladies' room, too.

"Hold the table while I go out to the parking lot to look for her," Salena told Karen.

Salena didn't think anything had been said or done to upset Jane, causing her to abandon them, and since she'd left her cell phone on the table, they couldn't call her to see what was taking so long.

Closing in on Jane's car, which was parked under a lamppost, Salena strained to see inside it. She got a sinking feeling in the pit of her stomach when she thought she could make out a figure slumped over the steering wheel. Breaking into a run, she dug inside her pocket for her cell phone, prepared to dial nine-one-one. It was exactly what she thought she was seeing, and she yanked open the door, thankful it was unlocked. She felt herself gag as she reached in to feel for a pulse, and then Jane's head rolled to the side when Salena touched her neck.

She fell backward, stumbling and telling herself, "No, no, no," over and over again. In tears, she dialed nine-one-one to report her friend's murder.

28

$\mathcal{H}$ was a good thirty minutes before Chad woke up, moaning in pain and blinking in confusion. His hand immediately went to his nose, which only inflicted more pain, causing shrill cries. It made Devin chuckle, causing Chad to jump in surprise and realize he had no idea where he was or who was with him—all he did know was that his nose was broken, and something very bad was happening or was about to happen.

He stumbled to his feet and instantly put his hands up in defense, causing another rupture of laughter from Devin. Chad's voice shook like a pubescent boy's. "Who the hell are you, and where the fuck am I?" he demanded while peering into the darkness trying to find help or at least a direction to run in.

Devin didn't answer right away; he wanted the arrogant punk to take it all in first. He had some nerve to shamelessly flirt with a woman like Salena as if he was even in her league.

Finally, he growled in a menacing voice, "I'm the one who hurt your pretty little nose that was poking where it didn't belong." He approached the frightened man, taking his time with slow strides.

Chad continued to hold his hands up, ready to throw a punch. He started backing up, though, while yelling, "What the fuck is going on?"

Devin smiled the most malevolent smile he could for Chad, and he knew it made chills run down the frightened man's spine because he saw him shiver.

Chad strained his eyes to see if he was really seeing what he thought he was. *Are those fangs? Who wears fangs?* Then he looked around himself again. He couldn't believe the enormous, intimidating stranger wanted to hurt him without even knowing why.

"What is this about? What do you have against me? I don't even know you, man," he yelped. Before getting his answers, though, he turned and bolted.

Devin counted to ten before going after the young man. Of course, it was no challenge for him to catch up to Chad; vampires were incredibly fast and incredibly strong. The movies at least got that part right. He grabbed him by his right shoulder and yanked him backward hard, causing him to fall flat on his ass. Then he grabbed the man's arm and pulled him back up with enough force to dislocate his shoulder.

Chad yelped in pain and tried to swing at his attacker, but his punch landed against what felt like a brick wall, and he was pretty sure he had broken fingers to top off his other injuries. He stumbled to get away but was pulled back against his attacker's massive form, and it knocked the wind out of him. Then he felt a steely arm tighten across his chest and begin to squeeze the air right out of him. As he struggled with every ounce of strength and willpower he had left, it didn't take him long to realize the arm was also squeezing the life right out of him, and there was no escaping. Yes, that realization came when he heard his ribs breaking and felt his lungs burning for air. He heard his back break also, and soon, all feeling below the neck was gone, and his arms and legs hung on him like spaghetti noodles. He was glad the agonizing pain was gone.

Just as the torture faded into the promising relief of darkness, he heard his killer say, "She's mine."

To emphasize his point, Devin bit into Chad's neck and ripped his throat out in one swift movement. He spit the blood out and left the corpse lying there for the scavengers. It was time to return to his truelove.

Salena woke up exhausted. Between being at the police station for an hour to provide her statement and then spending the rest of the night crying, she got maybe one to two hours of sleep. The police, trying to figure out if the crime was random or not, asked her if she knew of anyone who would want to hurt Jane and requested that she write down a grudge list for them. She came up blank so far.

She rubbed her temples, contemplating that Thursdays were always the busiest days at work. While grateful to still be on her vacation, she was thinking it certainly wasn't a good one. In fact, the historical home would have to manage without her for an additional week. She certainly had the time stored up. She called in and talked to Diane Burgess, her supervisor, and informed her she would not be returning to work on Monday after all. Diane was very understanding and told her to take as much time off as she needed to grieve.

She climbed out of bed and poured herself the strongest cup of coffee in her life. She grabbed a sheet of paper and a pen and, once again, tried to come up with the grudge list. However, she couldn't think of any enemies her friend may have had—no ex-lovers or friends came to mind that would hold a grudge against Jane. There certainly wasn't anyone who would want to kill her. *Was there?* Since none of Jane's belongings were missing, the crime didn't look like a random mugging, which is why the police wanted the grudge list. Her purse, briefcase, and CDs appeared untouched, but the police were still going to dust for prints.

Salena thought about the recent rash of murders and her own drama and tried to remember all the twisted details to find a connection to Jane's death. The one common trait that stuck out was that the female victims had bite marks—she looked down at her wrist but there was nothing there. Her fingers went to her neck, and she recalled that the mark there was already gone too. Part of her wanted to call the detective, who'd given her his business card, to ask if any had been found on Jane, but the other part of her wasn't so sure she wanted to know the answer—it might just be too horrible to comprehend. She was also curious if Jane had tested positive for signs of recent sexual activity since that was also a common factor among the female victims, including herself—well, sort of.

The detective had told her an autopsy would be performed, so she might as well wait to hear from him; he did promise to keep her informed. She looked at the business card again. *Okay, Detective Wagner, let's see you figure all this out.*

There was one phone call that she did make—she called Eric. She told him about Jane and asked him if he could make time to come back to New Orleans and escort her to the funeral service. Unfortunately, he was booked on a flight to London in the afternoon and would be gone for a week or two. He promised to visit her when he got back.

Mr. Dependable as always. She shouldn't have bothered. The other night didn't mean a thing to him. Hell, two years apparently didn't mean a thing to him. She didn't want to seem selfish, but in his line of work as a corporate attorney, he could've sent some lackey to London and came to New Orleans to be with her. Maybe she'd get a dog; they were more reliable.

A hot candlelight bath was beckoning her, so she gathered her towel, washcloth, and candles and headed into the bathroom for a relaxing soak—or so she thought. On the ledge of her garden tub was a vase full of white lilies—funeral flowers. She dropped her items and tugged her robe tightly closed as she ran back through her small house, checking the doors and windows—all were locked tight.

She knelt down and wept softly—more from confusion than fear, which was confusing in and of itself. No one had a key to her home, and she didn't leave a spare outside anywhere either. Even the police had said there was no sign of forced entry the last time, and none of her belongings had been missing. Feeling like her sanity was slowly slipping away, she bawled. Was Heloise right? Was she truly being stalked by a vampire? Vampire or not, the killer hadn't harmed her. Why was that? What did he want with her, and what was the connection with her grandmother? She needed answers. *She'd been home all morning too...*

Salena was on hold with the police station when she braved a trip back to the bathroom to examine the flowers. There was no card with the lilies, but she knew it had to be the same intruder as before—the mysterious man who got in and out with no trace. The same one who had seduced her and bit her twice now. *The vampire.*

She asked the operator to put her through to Officer Ann Marx since she'd investigated the first break-in. While on hold, feeling frightened that she may not be alone in her house, she locked the bathroom door, but she wondered what good it would do. Apparently, locks didn't hinder this person at all. *Hmm…person or vampire?*

"Are you alone, or is the intruder possibly still there?" Officer Marx asked her when she accepted the call.

"I honestly don't know, but all the doors and windows have been locked all day. I don't know how he got in again. I'm locked in the bathroom right now."

Officer Marx sighed under her breath, "That is strange." Then she added louder, "A unit is on its way. Stay in the bathroom with the door locked and grab anything that can be used as a weapon. Even a can of hairspray can do damage to the eyes. I'll stay on the line with you until the patrol officer gets there, and then I'll be on my way over as well."

Salena suddenly realized she could faintly smell the haunting musky scent again, right there in the bathroom, and it made her shiver—*mostly* from fear. Something still drew her in, and she had no idea why. How on earth could she be attracted to her stalker, slash mystery lover, slash vampire? But then again, Abigail had been...

A loud knock on the front door, followed by the shout, "Police!" about took ten years off her life. She ran to the front door to let the officer in while still holding the hairspray and only after looking through the peephole first.

Devin, while shifted into a black cat, marched around outside Salena's house, wondering if he'd made a mistake with the flowers. He'd watched her cry from his perch on her windowsill and felt horrible—especially since she'd been scared enough to call the police again. He'd meant to show his concern and condolences. He hadn't wanted to kill her friend, but the woman was going to interfere with their destiny.

He watched Salena say goodbye to the police. They'd only told her to make sure everything was always locked up tight and not to give out any spare keys. They also reminded her to get a lock put on the basement door, and to let them know if she noticed herself being followed or watched—including if anyone she was dating or had refused to date started acting out toward her. A crime scene tech had dusted for fingerprints, and Officer Marx said she'd let her know if anything showed up.

Salena was too shaken up to even notice one of the officers lean down to pet a black cat on his way back to the patrol car. She knew they thought she was crazy or just seeking attention. There was absolutely no proof someone had been in her home uninvited. Nothing had been tampered with, nothing was missing, and her locks were all fully functional. She suddenly started laughing hysterically, trying to imagine the looks on their faces if she told them she thought it was a vampire. They would definitely accuse her of being insane. Soon, her laughs turned into deep sobs.

After the officers were gone, Devin watched her close the door and heard the lock click. Then he ran to the side of her house where he watched her go into her bedroom, shut the door, and turn that lock as well. He had watched her come undone, and it hurt his heart.

She lay down in her inviting bed for a nap, which was an opportunity for him. He needn't worry about the locked doors and windows—he'd discovered an old pet door in the basement and used that to get in each time. He went up the basement stairs, as himself, and opened the door. The door had no lock, but it wouldn't have kept him out anyway. He quietly entered the kitchen and moved soundlessly like fog through the house to her bedroom. He shifted into a spider to crawl underneath the locked door. She was already sound asleep and snoring softly, so he changed back.

Devin slipped into bed with her, and she began to stir, but she didn't wake up. He watched her for several minutes, marveling at the beautiful softness in all her features—the features she'd inherited from Abigail. His dead heart beat faster, and his breaths came quicker as he imagined tracing his fingers, followed by his tongue, over her exquisite delicateness.

It was time. If his heart didn't tell him so, his rock-hardness certainly did. He was ready to seduce her completely. He began by brushing his fingertips across her cheek, and then he traced the fullness of her pouty lips.

That caused her sleepy eyes to flutter and slowly open. When she saw him, she quickly jerked away, but his body restrained her.

Devin stared hypnotically into her sky-blue eyes and whispered, "Nu vrei să lupte acest lucru. Vrei acest lucru." *You don't want to fight this. You want this.*

Salena's mouth, which had been open to scream, quickly closed. Her mind was trying to fight against the hypnotic trance, but it just couldn't seem to resist.

Devin quickly covered her mouth with his and plunged his tongue into it with bittersweet fervor, seeking her tongue. She wasn't resistant at all to the passionate tango that quickly engrossed her. He nibbled her lips and sucked on them gently which brought a soft moan of pleasure from her sweet mouth. His anxious hands, meanwhile, were moving up her soft body—cupping, squeezing, exploring—all the way up to stroke her silky strands of raven-black hair. It was the same hair he remembered from centuries ago, and he still loved its texture.

Feeling herself being accosted, drowning in an overwhelming passionate haze, Salena could only writhe underneath him in response. It was like her brain was stuck in cruise control, and her body could only ride along. She pushed herself against him and felt his aching bulge pressing against her slender thigh. This made her moist from anticipation. She had no way to fight against the tidal wave of desire pulling her under—every effort to resist was washed away with inevitability.

Devin responded to her hunger by pulling up her nightgown and plunging a finger into her hot, wet core— she was so velvety soft and tight, he thought he'd explode right then. While his finger expertly worked her insides, his mouth moved from hers, which was swollen from his kisses, to her neck. Just a taste—that's all he needed—this time. He nicked her alabaster skin just enough to cause a minuscule drop of blood to spill. He licked it up hungrily and absorbed her drugging nectar—traveling back almost three hundred years to his truelove. There was no denying their deep-rooted connection.

Worked up into a burning frenzy of lust, she didn't even notice the nick from his fangs. Instead, with a loud moan, she arched her body upward and grabbed his hand, urging it to go deeper. She used her other hand to rake her nails down his back, which was still concealed by his shirt, as he worked her pleasure point with his finger.

Not wanting to deny either of them their euphoria any longer, he moved his long virile body up the length of her. His fiery brand was released from its cotton confinement, and it eagerly prodded her hot, wet passage.

Salena cried out in pure bliss as he worked himself in and out of her petal-smooth opening until she stretched around him. Then every inch of her fiery furnace welcomed every inch of his steely staff.

As she rode the waves of ecstasy with him, her eyes rolled back, and she dug her teeth into his shoulder, which was an ironic change of pace for him.

However, before she could draw his blood, he stopped her. He captured her mouth and kissed her deeply again, moving his tongue in rhythm with his thrusts against the hard spot inside her womanhood. Prodding it made her explode in sensation all over his hard rod, and her nails once again dug into his back while she screamed even louder than before. This set him over the edge as well, and his white-hot eruption flooded into her convulsing center while she clutched his buttocks and rode the ripple of debauchery with him.

After removing his weight from her, he kissed the bite mark and then softly whispered in her ear, "Va dormi zdravăn acum." *You will sleep soundly now.*

He kissed her lips once more and headed back into the night. She was already snoring softly again by the time he left.

He wished he didn't have to hypnotize her to get her to make love and consummate their destiny. It hurt his heart that he couldn't just have her willingly.

"Soon," he declared to her through the darkness. "I will have all of you soon."

In what felt like days later, Salena finally woke up.
Her head was foggy, but her body was quite relaxed. She tried to remember the dream she'd had. *Was it a dream?* She couldn't be so certain anymore of what was real or not. She could smell musk in the air—his musk—and it blanketed her. She also felt sore in her most intimate place. Her doubts were erased—he had been there. But, like always, everything was still locked up. She needed to learn about the vampire and what was in store for her.

Two stops were necessary: the first was to see Heloise, and the second was to take a vampire tour. She got up to get ready and chose to take a quick hot shower over a bath. She wanted to scrub the musk off herself. It wasn't because she didn't find it pleasant; she actually liked it too much. As she washed, she remembered with a heavy heart a third stop she had to make. She needed to pay her respects to Jane's family. She cried in the stream of hot water pouring down on her. She was going to miss her friend terribly. Jane was the first friend she'd made when she moved to New Orleans.

She decided to call Detective Wagner for an update. He said he'd call, but she didn't want to wait on him. She needed to know who'd killed her friend. She hoped it wasn't the man she'd recently had passionate sex with—the vampire who was seeking her out because of her likeness to her great-grandmother.

"Hi, Detective Wagner. This is Salena Saunders," she greeted him with urgency in her voice. "I'm calling for an update on my friend's...um...murder." She had a hard time saying it aloud.

"Good morning, Miss Saunders. I've been busy with all the recent open cases, and that includes your friend's murder." She could hear him shuffling through papers on his desk. "You'd think it was Mardi Gras or something. That's when the crazy stuff usually happens.

"Okay, I've got her paperwork. Her autopsy showed that she died from a broken neck. There wasn't any evidence of sexual activity or bites on the body, unlike the other recent female victims. The only weapon used was a bare hand, which makes us believe it was definitely personal—someone had it in for her. Unfortunately, the prints lifted aren't in any database, and neither is the DNA swabbed from the bite marks on the other victims. So, and I hate to say this, we don't know who we are looking for. It could be the same perp or there could be more than one."

"So, what's next then?" she softly asked, feeling sick to her stomach again.

She heard more shuffling of papers on his end before he replied, "I just got some more reports back. The fingerprints from Miss Miller's case match up to some of the other murders, and Officer Marx just handed me the print results from the flower vase that was in your bathroom. It is also a match."

He paused, and she knew he was expecting her shocked reaction, but in truth, she wasn't shocked at all—except for maybe one thing. "You said *some* of the other murders. You're talking about the ones with the bite marks, right?"

Exhaustion from the unsolved cases was evident in his voice. "Yes, but only a handful of them. We have had a couple more since the weekend that are from a different doer. His prints and DNA aren't in the system either. The first killer left a couple of young men dead as well: one was Jeremy Tompkins, and other was just discovered by hiker yesterday. He was a missing waiter from Vincent's Italian Cuisine. I don't have the file in front of me, but I think his name was Chad.

"I have to admit, Miss Saunders, we are stumped on this one. But don't worry because we'll catch them. They will slip up or even turn on each other if they are working together. We think they are connected somehow because of the bite marks on most of the victims."

She heard more papers shuffling, and then he sighed loudly. "There *is* a connection—the DNA from the perps is a familial match," he announced in a tense voice.

"Oh fuck." She normally didn't swear, but it seemed appropriate at the moment. *Related vampires? Is there an entire family after me?*

He interrupted her horrifying thoughts. "Ma'am? He's been in your house, and we don't know how he is getting in. Is there somewhere else you can stay?" His voice was full of concern.

"No, I only had Jane to turn to. My other friend, Karen, who was with us that night, has her hands full with a husband, four kids, and three cats, which I'm allergic to. I don't really know anyone else, but I think I'll be okay." *He hasn't hurt me so far.*

The detective cleared his throat. "Well, if you can find someone else, I suggest you get out of your house immediately. There are always hotels. You're lucky to have survived this monster so far."

He's a monster all right. She touched her neck where she was bitten last. "Yes, I'm lucky," she whispered.

"I don't want you there if he decides to come back. You have my card if you need to call me. Take care." The line went dead.

Oh, he'll come back. Salena was sure of it.

After hanging up with the detective, Salena called Heloise to let her know that she needed to stop by. Heloise didn't answer her cell phone, though, and her voicemail box was full. Concerned, Salena headed to the woman's house to check up on her.

She arrived at Heloise's cottage about fifteen minutes later and saw the woman's sedan parked in the driveway. She hurried to the door and knocked loudly but received no response.

Feeling even more concerned, she peeked inside the windows and called out to her friend, "Heloise, are you in there? It's Salena." Finally, she heard movement, and she saw Heloise walking toward the door. "I was worried about you there for a minute. You didn't answer your phone or the door," Salena explained with her words rushed together.

"Sorry, dear. I was taking a nap. You know how it is at my age. Now, what's wrong?"

Salena didn't quite know where to start. "Well, it's about the vampire. My best friend was murdered, and someone has been breaking into my house, and..." she wasn't sure about finishing her sentence. She looked away in shame from the woman's appraising stare. "I think he seduced me," she quietly rambled after a long pause.

"Well," Heloise sighed and shrugged. "That is the way he was described in my great-grandmother's diary. That is the way of the vampire, and he's probably the one in your house because he wants you. Originally, I thought your life was in danger, but if it was, he would've made a move already to harm you. I think he sees Abigail when he looks at you. As for the other matter, I'm so sorry about your friend. But you don't think it was him, do you?"

Salena began sobbing and paced quickly around the small parlor room. "The police said the fingerprints matched the prints found in my house, so, yes, it was him. Why? Why would he kill my friend and then bring me flowers to make it better? He left funeral flowers in my bathroom. I swear, Heloise, I'm going to go insane from this."

The Gypsy peered at her over her reading glasses and frowned. "That is odd. I'm not sure what to make of it."

Salena started biting her nails again; she was almost to the quick on a few of them. "I don't know what to think anymore. Vampires are supposed to be make-believe, but then the police tell me there is another suspect in similar murders, and it's a familial match to him. So, is a family of vampires hunting me?"

Heloise's eyes widened in surprise. "I had no idea about that. Of course, this is New Orleans, and I've always known that the dead walk among us."

Salena threw her hands up. "Then why don't the cops know that too? Why aren't they crying vampire?" she squawked.

Heloise wrung her withered hands. "Well, not everyone believes in the paranormal. Sometimes, you have to let go of your system of beliefs to accept what is right in front of you. Look at me. How many people really believe I can see the future?"

Salena shook her head. "I don't know. Can we look at the cards again?" She was still trying to hold out hope that this was all some colossal joke. Jane would really be alive, no vampires would be coming after her, and the passionate encounters would have been just dreams. *Damn good dreams.*

"Yes, let's have another look."

Heloise soon had three shuffled decks and Salena chose three cards. They were the same as before—Death, Fool, and Tower—so she picked the decks up and looked through all the cards to make sure there were different ones and, of course, there were. Then she had Heloise shuffle once more, and this time the Gypsy picked the three cards for her. They were the same, though.

Heloise once again pointed out the possibility of danger. "I'm still not certain what to make of this, but I know it's not good. I don't think it's the one who is reminded of Abigail who would do you harm. There has to be another—perhaps the family member who is also killing. You must be careful, Salena. Keep your eyes open to that danger while you keep your heart open for the one who desires you. Now, I must end our visit. I need to check up on a friend in the hospital." She walked Salena out and drove off to see her friend, while Salena stared in shock after her.

When she could will her feet to move again, Salena climbed into her car and headed back to New Orleans to check out a vampire tour for the very first time.

Salena found out that the next vampire tour wouldn't begin until 8:30 p.m., and it would last two hours. She prepaid for her ticket and grabbed a brochure to read.

Back home, after reading the brochure—filled with intrigue and spookiness—she decided to do some internet research on vampire myths. Bringing up her internet browser, she typed *vampire myths and legends* into the search engine. While the results loaded, she glanced at her painting, thinking she should finish it soon, but something was off—something was different. She thought about the other night when she'd worked on it to relax. She had worked on the swan, not the fountain; however, it was finished. She stared closely at the fountain and the broad, heavy brush strokes—they were definitely different from the small, delicate strokes she painted with.

So, the one who gets in and out of my house like a ghost is also artistic.

She admired the perfect curves and detail of the fountain. He'd done a remarkable job on it. Then she looked around her tidy house, wondering what else he had touched and, again, how he was getting in. She had to find out—especially before he assaulted her again.

Is it assault if you enjoyed it?

Shaking her head at the complex mess her life had become lately, she turned her attention back to the computer screen. Her search results had finally loaded. She clicked on the first link available, and it took her to legends from Europe. They were typical stories of the undead drinking the blood of helpless victims in the middle of the night. She read the myths about crucifixes, garlic, caskets, sunlight, and holy water. She scoffed at those—he'd left the lilies during the daytime, and she had a crucifix hanging above her bed. Also, there was the garlic butter she had put on her seafood the other night. She grimaced—it was the night Jane was killed. Speaking of Jane, why didn't he drink her blood? Since when do vampires break necks? Maybe it was someone else who had killed her. She briefly felt relieved from the thought.

Wait. No, the detective had said the prints matched the flower vase. It had to be him.

She found it strange that she would want to exonerate a vampire. If he was in fact a vampire—she still wasn't sure she believed. But, what other explanation was there? Was he just a man with a biting fetish? But then why do the bite marks suddenly disappear?

She wondered if she should tell the detective why his fingerprints weren't in the database. *You won't find them, Detective Wagner, because he is, oh, at least three hundred years old. Do you have any wooden stakes? Yeah, that'd go over really well,* Salena mused to herself.

She looked at a few more links from her search. It was just more of the same—including if a person survived a bite, they'd turn into a vampire. So far, she didn't think she was one. She wasn't craving blood; she was only craving answers.

She looked at her family tree, which was still spread out. How could her tenth-generation great-grandmother love a vampire? Was it because of the seduction? It was affecting *her* after all. Was she going to fall in love with the monster too? She needed to know.

There were some references to vampires in the U.S.—particularly in New Orleans. Mostly, though, it was just advertisement for the various vampire tours. Next, she searched for vampires falling in love. She didn't find any love stories involving vampires in the U.S.; she only read a couple of stories about suspected romances in Europe. The stories spoke of women falling in love with the most handsome and charming of men who only appeared at night. Shortly after the men came into their lives, though, the women were found dead and drained of their blood. They would then disappear from the morgue or their abandoned graves. They'd become part of the undead and would wander the streets at night, seeking fresh blood.

"Gee, that's exactly what I'm looking for," Salena exclaimed to the empty room before shutting down her computer.

Looking at her watch, she decided it was time to go to the funeral home. Since the autopsy was finished, Jane's body was released to the funeral home and was going to be laid out that evening. Her parents wanted the services sooner rather than later, so they could bury their daughter. She quickly changed into a suitable black dress and headed out, with her eyes already swimming in tears.

On her front porch, she found a black cat. She was certain it was the same one from before that had caused her to burn herself. As if to apologize, it went right for her leg, rubbing and purring.

"Shoo!" she told it, but it didn't budge.

She grabbed the broom that she kept on the porch and swatted at it, but it still sat there, purring and looking up at her.

"Whatever," she grumbled before walking off.

At the bottom of the steps, however, she turned and looked at the cat again. It was the same one from the night Eric was there, she was certain of it, but could it be the same one from the farmer's market? That was about six or seven miles from her house, so how could it be? She shook her head and climbed into her car.

At the funeral home, Salena talked with Jane's friends and family. She'd met Jane's parents only once, but they both remembered her. Their overwhelming grief mixed with hers and brought on a new onslaught of tears. She didn't know any of Jane's co-workers, and Rob, whom Jane had wanted to fix her up with, wasn't there. She overheard someone say he had sent his condolences, but he was too ill to make it to the service.

It's just as well. This isn't exactly an appropriate place to meet men.

Soon, it was time for the vampire tour, and she found herself shaking. She was afraid of what she'd discover there.

35

Salena got in line with several thrilled tourists. She was probably the only one who didn't look excited. She was there for answers but was, admittedly, afraid to hear them. She assumed she'd probably only find more myths, resulting in more questions.

The tour guide, a tall and dark man named Clive, was completely in character. He was wearing a long black cape over his eighteenth-century attire and plastic fangs—at least Salena hoped they were plastic. His ensemble reminded her of a photo she'd seen online while doing her research. Apparently, Clive had done his research as well.

He addressed his audience in a spooky vampire voice. "How many vampires do we have with us tonight?"

A few costumed individuals raised their hands, and laughter erupted from the others. Clive looked at all of them with a grave expression.

"Now how many *real* vampires do we have here tonight? If you dare to reveal yourselves that is," he said with a wink.

Everyone looked around the group, and slowly, a few people raised their hands, causing more laughter—especially when Clive declared, "Well, please don't eat any of us tonight."

He waved his arm in a grand gesture and bowed to the group. Then, while looking into their excited faces, he asked, "Shall we?"

They proceeded to walk slowly down the dark streets of the French Quarter. With no moon or stars visible in the overcast sky, it was pitch-black out. Clive, however, seemed used to the darkness, while everyone else bumped into each other and stumbled over pits and cracks in the quiet street.

Salena could see fog rolling in their direction, and it added to the eeriness of the evening. As they pressed forward, she smelled garlic on the couple walking beside her.

They must be believers. If they only knew...

As they traveled the haunted streets, Clive regaled them with some vampire history—particularly how they came to New Orleans. He enthralled the group with the story of the "Casket Girls" from the eighteen hundreds. He shared the account of how French families sent their daughters to New Orleans to marry. Supposedly, the girls brought trousseaus with them which were casket shaped, giving the girls their nickname. When the girls were matched to suitors, the trousseaus were presented to the men, but they were empty. It was rumored that vampires had been smuggled to the French Quarter inside them.

"So, watch out!" Clive hissed, bringing his hands, adorned with long vampire fingernails, up to his chest and showing off his fangs. "Vampires might be prowling nearby—especially in one of the vampire taverns." He gave them an eerie laugh, which seemed to bounce off the streets and dark buildings.

Surprised, Salena found she was actually enjoying the tour and its theatrics. She wasn't sure if the anecdote was real or not, but she certainly liked the way Clive presented it. Unfortunately, she didn't see who was enjoying her.

36

Gabriel ran his tongue over his fangs. *This is too easy*. He blended into the tourist group and followed closely behind a woman with midnight-black hair. She was his chosen prey. She was a beautiful creature, and he could smell the honeysuckle and lavender scent radiating from her skin. Oddly, it took him back to Abigail; he could vividly remember her always smelling like that too. In fact, this creature was just as enticing as Abigail had been— *someone you can really sink your teeth into*. He watched the soft sway of her hips as she walked. Her curves were sexy as hell, and he couldn't help but imagine taking her from behind with his hands on her hips, driving her hard and making her squeal with gratification. He would definitely use her for his self-indulgence before sinking his fangs into her soft shoulder and drinking every drop of her blood, and he would enjoy every single lascivious minute of it.

Salena followed the group into a famed vampire tavern to check it out. There definitely was a sinister group of men and women in there, but, thankfully, it was a small one. She tried to avoid eye contact with them, especially when she heard a few low growls. The sound reminded her of the low growls from her mystery lover; although, his hadn't been threatening sounds. They'd been inviting sounds of pure pleasure. Blushing from the heated memory, she kept her eyes on the backs of those walking in front of her.

Gabriel didn't avoid eye contact at all. He stared all the posers down. The men put up a front until he got closer and gave them a growl of his own; then they backed down in obvious fear. The women watched him appreciatively. Naturally, a woman pretending to be a vampire would desire an *actual* vampire.

Scrutinizing the posers, he could sense that one of them wasn't faking it. He looked them over one-by-one, breathing in their essences and looking into their eyes—all had black eyes, but someone wasn't wearing contacts. He found the one, a blond woman, who was the real deal. They smiled equally sinister grins at each other, and Gabriel put his finger to his lips.

She nodded in return—they'd keep each other's secret. Gabriel could tell she'd picked out the man two seats down from her by the way she kept looking at him. Then she stood up and approached Gabriel, looking from him to Salena and then back to him again.

She whispered in his ear, "I'd do her," and smiled a venomous smile. Walking out, the beautiful vampire tapped her dinner on his shoulder, and they left together, no questions asked.

Gabriel's second choice of prey followed him outside. One of the posers was about to get her wish—to meet a real vampire up close and personal.

Figuring he'd give the tour group a real vampire show, he pushed his groupie up against the wall and bit savagely into her neck. Her scream caught everyone's attention, and they were transfixed. The blood dripping down her blouse brought cheers and applause. Then, when he turned toward them, licking his lips and rubbing his belly while she slumped to the pavement, the crowd went crazy with excitement.

One person didn't cheer, though—Salena could tell it wasn't a performance. And while he was tall, dark, and devastatingly handsome, he wasn't her mysterious vampire. Maybe he was the other one Detective Wagner spoke about. Maybe he was the familial match. She trembled in fear.

I could solve these crimes for them easily, but would they believe me? She guessed not.

Gabriel bowed over the dead woman and was about to get back into line with the group, when he could smell something in the air—Devin. His brother was getting close. Maybe he'd decided to hunt in the same area. Gabriel was looking forward to the family reunion, but he wasn't about to let his main course get away. He'd find his brother after his appetite was satiated.

A man approached Gabriel while he was scanning the dark for Devin. "Hey," the clueless man greeted him. "That was so cool! It looked so real!" He held his hand out for a shake, and Gabriel glanced at it with distaste.

While staring into the man's brown eyes with his midnight-black ones, he took the hand and squeezed hard. He could have crushed it, and normally he would have, but Devin's scent was getting stronger, and fog was blanketing the night. If he wanted to make his move on the woman, it was the right time.

The man gasped in pain, "Wow, dude, you are really strong." He could barely get the words out.

Gabriel snarled, dropped the man's hand, and fell back into the creeping fog.

Salena watched him vanish, whereas the others were chattering about the show they'd just witnessed. She felt it was strange that no one was checking on the lifeless looking woman, still lying on the ground. She didn't need to check and was about to make an anonymous call to the police when the fog crept upon her as well. It was so thick, she couldn't even see inside her bag to grab her cell phone. But something, or rather *someone*, grabbed her.

Salena tried to scream, but a large hand was covering her mouth as the enormous person dragged her away from the crowd. She couldn't see anything in front of her or the person behind her, but she felt herself pressed up against a large, rock-hard body, and she was being held with an iron grip. She wondered if this was the end for her, and Jane entered her thoughts. She had no idea who had her, but since she'd seen a vampire in their tour group and had watched him kill already, she safely assumed it was him. Part of her was relieved that it wasn't her mystery lover.

Just as she thought she was about to die—since she was several feet away from the tour group, and they were oblivious to the abduction—she heard a shout and was knocked to the ground.

Putting her hands and knees into motion, Salena scrambled through the impenetrable fog as fast as she could move. She felt cuts from sharp rocks as they dug into her delicate flesh, but it didn't matter. Every drop of her adrenaline was pumping and forcing her to keep moving away from the vampire. Then her hopes were once more dashed as she felt herself being grabbed yet again. The grip, however, was gentler, and the hand over her mouth was warmer and softer.

Her captor whispered to her, "It's all right. I have you now, and you are safe with me. I *swear* I'm not going to harm you."

His voice was deep, familiar, and extremely sexy; however, he could promise her the moon and everything under it, and she still wouldn't trust him. The word "vampire" somewhat said it all, and she fought hard to break free from his hold. Her efforts were futile, though, because he didn't loosen his grip.

Devin turned her around to look at her beautiful face. As soon as he removed his hand, and she was about to scream, he plunged his tongue into her mouth and kissed her with all the passion in his soul.

Salena's scream was stifled by a firm tongue that seemed to be searching her mouth for acceptance. Then she noticed the musky fragrance for the first time. It was *him*. Panicked, she bit down as hard as she could, and as soon as he let go in pain, she ran. The fog had begun to lift enough for her to see a short distance in front of herself, and she ran to her car as fast as her legs could carry her.

Devin watched her flee. He was in pain from the bite, but he didn't blame her; Gabriel had terrified her. The fog had carried a scent to Devin when he was looking for Salena. It wasn't just any scent, though, it was someone from his past—his brother, Gabriel.

He was utterly relieved that he'd gotten there just in time to stop his brother. Gabriel had been ready to sink his teeth in when Devin had knocked him out of the way. Gabriel got away from him, but at least Salena was safe. Devin couldn't sense his brother's presence anywhere. Well, anywhere but on a dead body he came across. He could smell Gabriel's scent on the lifeless woman, whose body was lying near a pile of garbage.

He gazed into the fog with deep concern on his face. Why did his brother suddenly show up there after so much time had passed? More importantly, why did he go after Salena? There were several women in that tour group.

Concerned, Devin left in search of his love. He had to be there to protect her.

Gabriel got away, but barely. He was so close too. He was just about to sink his fangs into the tasty woman's neck when his brother intervened. This made him wonder if Devin had been after him or the beautiful prey—he'd have to find out.

Well, at least now Devin knew he was back. That should make things interesting. Still famished, he roamed the French Quarter in search of prey. He may not have gotten the dark-haired woman, but there were plenty of others to choose from, and he wouldn't stop with just one.

During the mad dash to her car, Salena's thoughts about what had just happened to her screamed in her head. While she couldn't see anything in the thick fog, she knew her first captor was the same man—or vampire—who had killed the woman while everyone watched. She replayed the horrible scene in her mind. The way he'd smiled, a purely heinous smile, with the woman's blood running down his chin while he bowed to his audience gave her chills. *Yes, he's a vampire. There, I said it. I guess I do believe.* Her admission made tears flood her eyes, and it made her run faster.

Why was everyone she consulted telling her that a monster was part of her future? Even if her mystery lover had saved her from the other, how could she accept her fate with him? Nothing was rational.

As she ran passed some shops to her car, which was in sight, someone grabbed her again, and she screamed.

The Gypsy holding her arm shook it and told her, "Madame Zoyla knows what you seek, and I can help you." She gave Salena a very stern expression. "You need to contact *her* for answers." She tugged on Salena's arm again. "Come inside. Your answers are in here, and it's safe."

Salena reluctantly went with the eager Gypsy. She didn't think vampires would follow her inside a Gypsy's lair, so it probably was a safe place for her—especially if the first vampire was still lurking around.

Madame Zoyla locked the door and then lit the candles around a table in the center of the room. She motioned for Salena to have a seat at the table.

"What is this about?" Salena asked while sitting down.

Madame Zoyla sat down across from her and replied, "We will contact the woman with whom it all began. Tell me her name."

Salena was stunned and confused. "I don't know whom you're talking about."

The Gypsy was demanding. "She is the one who had his love first. It's the love he seeks now with you."

Recognition finally dawned on her. "Oh! You are talking about my great-grandmother, Abigail. Her name is…I mean was… Abigail Saunders."

"Great. We will contact her spirit and get your answers. Take my hands."

Salena took her hands, which felt hotter than lava. She had never done a séance before, so she felt uneasy. She curiously watched as Madame Zoyla closed her eyes and began to slowly rock back and forth. She started mumbling something under her breath that Salena couldn't understand, but then she spoke clearly.

"Abigail Saunders, pass over to our side and come into me to speak to your grandchild. She has questions only you can answer."

Again, she rocked back and forth and mumbled something Salena didn't understand. Then she opened her dark eyes with a sad expression.

"She can't come into me because I can't connect with those who died so tragically. They don't completely let go of the earthly plane. I'm so sorry," she declared.

Salena dropped the woman's hands. "Well, she was burned alive for allegedly being a witch."

Madame Zoyla looked shocked. "Oh my, that is tragic! Unfortunately, the biggest tragedy, though, is a lost love—one that is unfulfilled."

Salena considered that and spoke her thoughts aloud. "Yes, she fell in love with a vampire, and then she was burned alive because of it."

"Vampire? That does explain things then." The woman looked deeply into Salena's eyes. "If a vampire falls in love, it's a monumental love, and the bonds are never broken. It's eternal just like the vampire. It's a magical spell that is very rare. I can understand now." She clasped the evil eye pendant hanging from a chain around her neck. "He has rediscovered her in you through your blood ties. Let me see your palm, girl."

Salena slowly presented her hand for a reading.

"Yes, look here," Madame Zoyla continued. "These two long lines have a third line intersecting right here"—she pointed it out to Salena—"The two are the vampire and your great-grandmother, and here you are as the third line that joins the longer of the first two. Here you are joined with the vampire." With that, she dropped Salena's hand and abruptly stood up. "You must leave now. I sense evil is near, and I don't want danger in my home. Go, please! Go to the one who loves you because only he can protect you."

Startled that evil was near, which she immediately assumed was the other vampire, Salena bolted from the shop. She rarely drove over the speed limit, but it felt necessary to do so. At home, she checked each lock three times—even the one in the creepy basement.

Salena woke up with the early morning sun glaring into her still half-closed eyes. She had nightmares all night long about bloodsuckers. It wasn't even just vampires; there were also mosquitoes and leeches. With a little early morning humor, she wondered why lawyers weren't in the mix. It was Saturday and the day of Jane's funeral. Getting up, she started the coffee pot and a hot shower. She never noticed the black crow in the windowsill, but it definitely noticed her.

Jane's funeral was packed with friends and family. Salena smiled as she thought about how Jane always liked being surrounded by her loved ones. Tears pooled in her eyes as she looked around at their remorseful faces.

The service was lovely, and the procession headed to a peaceful cemetery. As she watched the internment, Salena felt like she was being watched herself. She looked around, but everyone's face was where it should be—on Jane's coffin. She didn't see the black crow watching her from the nearby treetops, and neither did the man who was approaching her.

Salena jumped when someone grabbed her elbow. She looked up into a kind smile and soft brown eyes.

"You're Salena Saunders, right?" the man asked.

"Yes. Do I know you?" she inquired with an arched brow.

"Not yet, and I'm sorry to meet under these circumstances. I'm Rob," he explained and held out his hand.

She shook his hand and returned his smile. Then so he wouldn't mistake it as interest, she quickly looked away and dropped his hand.

He cleared his throat and asked, "Would you like to have dinner later? We could share memories of Jane."

Salena mumbled, "I don't know." She had way too much weird stuff going on to think about dating, even if he was a mortal.

Just then, a black crow dove at him. Rob jumped backward while waving his arms wildly in the air and tripped over a large tree stump, falling on his butt. The bird continued to attack him, leaving cuts on his hands and face from its talons. Salena jumped in to shoo the riled bird away, but it didn't fly too far. Instead, it perched itself in the tree directly above them and watched Rob with its beady black eyes.

Rob gathered himself up off the ground, and while quickly walking backward, he gave Salena a shaky wave.

"Sorry, but I'll have to catch up with you another time," he remarked.

While she watched, stunned, the bird took one more dive at Rob as he walked to his car.

Salena headed home immediately after Rob's bizarre bird attack. She supposed his cologne had set the crow off. In any case, she'd definitely had more than her nerves could handle for one day, and it was time to say a final goodbye to her dear friend and go home. She gave a hug to Jane's parents and left a single rose on the grave. She would miss her dear friend terribly.

When she got home, she thought of her blood-sucking intruder and decided not to go inside—not yet. She sat on the top step, surrounded by colorful pots of flowers, and rested her head up against a column. Her tears fell softly until something brushed against her back, causing her to shriek and jump up with her arms thrashing. It was the black cat, and it kept pressing against her in spite of her reaction.

"Shoo, get out of here," she scolded the feline while pushing it away.

Between all the flowers at the funeral and the cat dander, her eyes started to itch, and she began sneezing.

The cat stopped rubbing, looked at her with sad eyes, and trotted off—but just to the corner of her porch.

Trying to brush the fur off herself, Salena rose to go inside and seek some allergy medicine. As she got up, a breeze came through and carried with it the familiar and alluring musky scent. Frightened, she stared at her front door ominously. Should she go in? Would she be safe in her own home? She didn't really have a choice—she had nowhere else to go. She had no family nearby, and her best friend was gone. Feeling abandoned, a floodgate of tears opened up, and the cat responded with soft mewling. It was watching her come undone. She looked at the cat with a tilt of her head.

"Well, what do you think, boy? Is it safe?"

The cat once again approached her, and against her better judgment, she bent down and scratched it between the ears. It certainly was an odd animal, always showing up the way it did. Despite her allergies, she went inside and got some chicken from the fridge to feed the cat. The stray was quite grateful.

"So, am I stuck with you, boy? You can't come inside, and I've never really had a pet before, so don't expect much." The exceedingly loud purr and forceful rub against her leg told her he didn't mind. *Are you a boy?* She picked the animal up to check. "Yep, you're a boy," she confirmed to the cat.

You're just another strange male creature in my life now.

After checking the house for an intruder, not that she knew what to do if she'd found one, Salena changed her clothes and put the ones she had been wearing into the wash. She thought about the stray cat. It was strange that it was hanging around because she had never seen any cats in the neighborhood before. She was sure she would be seeing it from then on, though, since she'd fed it. Like it or not, she had a new pet. She walked to the refrigerator and wrote "cat food" on her shopping list.

Her stomach reminded her that she'd not eaten yet, so she rummaged in the refrigerator for some leftover pasta. She had no idea she was being watched through the kitchen window; a black crow sat on the windowsill watching her every move.

Lost in thought while grabbing salad ingredients from the crisper, she jumped and bumped her head when her cell phone rang. She was sure her heart had stopped beating for a second.

"Hello?" she answered while rubbing the bump that was already forming.

A male voice she didn't recognize greeted her. "Hi, Salena. It's Rob."

Surprised, she answered, "Rob, hi. How are you? Are you okay? I was worried about you after—" she trailed off, not wanting to embarrass him further.

"Yeah," he replied sheepishly. "That was strange, wasn't it? Crazy damn bird."

After an awkward silence, she asked him, "So...um...how'd you get my number?"

"Oh," he began cautiously, "I got it from Jane before...you know. I'm still hoping you'll agree to have dinner with me." He laughed nervously. "I hope the incident with that insane bird didn't ruin my chances."

"Well, I don't know if that's a good idea right now," she mumbled.

She stared at the floor, trying to think of an excuse, when she was startled by a noise outside her window. She glanced over, saw black wings flapping wildly against the window, and dropped her phone. It was a black crow. Until very recently, she wasn't used to seeing them around.

"Just like the cat..." she whispered to herself while chills ran up and down her spine.

"Hello? Salena, are you still there?" she heard coming from the floor.

She picked the phone up and told him, "Yes, I'm here. I have butter fingers and dropped my phone." She looked back toward the window, but the bird was already gone.

Rob cleared his throat and pressed, "Salena, I know you're grieving, but can we have dinner tonight at 7:00? I'd really like to get to know you better."

"Um...I don't know if I'm ready." She kept her eyes fixed on the window, but there was nothing there.

"I know you're upset," he said softly, "and I want to help you if I can. It's just dinner with no expectations."

Salena didn't want to hurt his feelings, and she didn't think he was going to give up, so she agreed. "Okay, pick me up at The Edgar Degas House at 7:30. I have to pick up some papers there anyway."

The truth was, she didn't want to invite him to her house and be expected to invite him inside. She already had one man in and out of her house without her desire or consent. Then as she hung the phone up, a chilling thought occurred to her—what if Rob was the one who was scaring her, stalking her, and making her afraid to be in her own home? It would certainly make more sense than the vampire theory. Then again, what about what she'd witnessed during the vampire tour? There was no denying that. Also, he didn't look like her mystery lover at all unless he somehow changed his appearance to blend in.

She needed more answers; Heloise would just have to see her before her date.

42

Devin perched outside Salena's window. He was out of sight but not out of earshot. He heard Salena agree to meet the man, whom she addressed as Rob, for dinner, and he would just have to intervene.

He peered inside and watched her nervously pacing through her small house while biting her fingernails. He wished he could put her fingertips in his mouth. First, he would plant soft kisses on them, and then he would suck on them gently, and finally, he would nibble on them ever so slightly to make her body shiver from desire. His little bird heart fluttered wildly as he imagined feeling her body writhing underneath him again. She'd felt so good—so perfect—when they'd made love.

Suddenly pulled from his daydream, Devin saw her pick up her cell phone, and with shaking hands, she typed in a number.

Her voice trembled when she spoke to the other person. "Heloise, can I come visit you?" she asked, and then she listened in. "Okay, I'll be right there. Bye." She hung up and grabbed her purse, rushing out the door.

Salena quickly left for Heloise's house. It was raining, so travelling down the curvy highway wasn't something to look forward to. It was just a light sprinkle at first, but just as she was backing out of her driveway, it turned into a downpour. Through the deluge, she didn't see the black wolf running alongside the woods, keeping pace with her car.

Chilled, Salena reached over to adjust the heater. Her eyes were off the road for only a second, but that is all it took. Regretfully, she hadn't noticed the huge puddle of standing water in the road. Her car hit it and caused her to hydroplane. In a panic, she overcorrected her steering wheel and slid off into the ditch. It scared her to death, but she wasn't hurt. The car seemed to be okay too. She was thankful that it was a ditch and not a tree.

After she collected her wits, she tried to pull out of the ditch but couldn't because the rain was coming down harder and faster, and the tires were stuck in the mud. After spinning the tires and figuring she was making matters worse, she turned the engine off and grabbed her cell phone to call for a tow.

Just as she began to dial, though, she felt the car shake. She dropped the phone in a panic and tried desperately to see out the rain-streaked windows; however, everything was blurred. She felt the car moving on its own and gripped her seat and steering wheel so tightly, her knuckles turned white. She didn't follow any particular religion, but she said a silent prayer.

Suddenly, there was a soft thud, and the car stopped moving. The rain had let up just enough for her to catch a glimpse of a shadow moving across the back window—a large shadow. Thankfully, it was moving away from the car. After she felt safe and had worked up her nerve, she looked out the window again and couldn't believe her eyes—she was back on the road! *How the hell did that happen?* Feeling very disturbed, yet extremely relieved, she felt the best course of action would be to get out of there as quickly as possible.

Despite the wet roads, Salena hastened the rest of the way to Heloise's house.

I must have a guardian angel.

Devin was glad he had been there for Salena when she had needed him. He had wanted to knock on her car window, help her out of the vehicle, and take her into his arms to assure her all would be okay. Of course, he knew that wouldn't have gone over too well. She wasn't ready yet.

Shifted back into a massive black wolf, he raced closer to the road just in case Salena needed him again.

Unfortunately, his intense focus on her kept him from noticing the brown wolf watching from one-hundred yards away.

Gabriel had seen Devin's heroism; he'd seen everything because he'd followed his brother and the tasty morsel. He'd been following them since the vampire tour.

He saw a definite resemblance between this woman and Devin's last love, Abigail, which must be why Devin was interested in anything other than a meal from her. She'd even smelled like her last night, but in the dark, he hadn't noticed the striking physical similarities. Yes, he was aware of what his brother was up to; he'd kept a close eye on him and the woman all day.

Gabriel closed his black eyes and smiled sensually as he remembered the luscious, enticing Abigail. He knew he would have her, all of her, but then something interfered—his older brother. Devin had fallen for the mortal, and since Gabriel had only planned to use her for his appetites, he didn't feel like challenging his brother for her. Truth be told, he hadn't thought he would've won that fight. He'd always felt it was useless to take a mate—especially a mortal one—when there was all eternity for him to sample different flavors, and he certainly wouldn't give that up to be mortal again!

The stealthy brown wolf raced to catch up to the car and his long-lost brother while remaining hidden. Devin should've noticed his presence to begin with—his skills must be thrown off by his obsession with the mortal. Well, that would all work in Gabriel's favor—not that he was worried about facing Devin anymore. He'd become a much stronger vampire than he used to be. He even had some new maneuvers that he couldn't wait to use.

Salena's heart was still pounding loud and hard in her ears when she pulled into the driveway at Heloise's small cottage. Rushing to get inside, she failed to notice the black cat in the windowsill and the brown owl in a nearby tree. The owl, however, did notice the cat and thought, at least for a second, that the cat noticed him too.

Devin perched in the windowsill and watched Salena rush inside. She was still trembling, and that made him sad. He meowed out of concern, but she didn't notice. The swift rain breeze caught Salena's wonderful fragrance of lavender and honeysuckle but also another faint and familiar scent. He looked around for Gabriel, but then a loud voice inside the cottage caught his attention.

He overheard the Gypsy woman exclaim, "Salena, you're in danger! Come and sit down. We must look at the cards again."

Salena sat down next to Heloise on her small sofa. "Yes, I know I'm in danger. I ran off the road on the way here. I'm in danger from myself. My hands are still shaking. Look." She held her hands up to emphasize.

Heloise was surprised. "Well, I'm glad to see you weren't hurt, but I'm afraid this is worse than that."

"Great," Salena sighed, rolling her beautiful blue eyes. "Lay it on me."

Heloise shuffled the tarot cards and placed them in front of Salena on the coffee table while telling her, "I had a dream about you last night, but I don't think it was just a dream. I think it was a vision—a vision of evil forces battling over you. There was a sinister shadow around you. Let's see if I'm right."

"Wow. Can this day get any better?" Salena asked sarcastically.

Heloise told Salena to choose four cards. She laid the first three cards on the table in front of Salena, and then she placed the fourth card horizontally across the top of them. Her aged eyes, full of insight and disquiet, looked at Salena as she flipped over the first card.

"That card is Judgement in the reversed position. That means it represents trouble from the past; however, it might not be yours. It might be in your bloodline, or…" she hesitated and then whispered, "it might be your past life if you believe in such things." Giving Salena a wink, she continued to examine the card. "Now, the picture of people falling out of their coffins represents something ominous. It looks like the dead are rising."

"Well, we are talking about a vampire, right?" Salena interrupted.

"Yes, but I don't think it's the one who adores you. Someone else from the past–likely from Abigail's time–is haunting you. That's what I'm concerned about." She looked at Salena with a worried expression. "This pile"— she tapped the second stack and flipped the card— "represents the present. This card is The Lovers. Your soulmate is near." She looked at Salena with a curiously sentimental grin, but Salena just shook her head.

"I don't even date anymore," she said under her breath. "And I would never date a vampire, so you can stop smiling like that's good news."

Heloise laughed lightly.

"Besides, he was my great-grandmother's love, not mine."

"Might be one and the same. After all, gypsies do believe in reincarnation. That's why our magic is strong; we are born with the knowledge." Heloise turned over the third and fourth cards simultaneously and sighed. "The Six of Cups and The Devil. These represent your future, but they also refer to the history of you and your soulmate."

Salena huffed, "You mean my vampire? He's The Devil card, right?"

"Not necessarily. Someone was seriously harmed in the past, and there is a karmic debt to settle before the lovers can make their way back to one another and consummate their bonds of truelove. But The Devil card serves as a warning—something from the past will try to interfere, just as before. Something will try to stop the lovers again."

Salena jumped up from the sofa and screeched, "Do you mean like another vampire?"

"It would appear so, but I think your truelove will protect you."

Salena massaged her temples as a migraine came on. She thought back to the flowers and her dream. "I don't understand this," she said with tiredness in her eyes and voice. "A week ago, I had a normal life with a career, healthy friends, and no drama. Now—" she couldn't finish the sentence.

Heloise took her hand and squeezed it gently. "Salena, we'll figure this out. We know that there are mystical forces in your life right now. They are the same ones that were in your great-grandmother's from so long ago. Unfortunately, that causes uncertainty. I still see love, but the danger, which is measurable, is also present."

"What does that mean?" The question came out more like a shout.

"It means there are conflicting forces at work right now that haven't been resolved, and I cannot determine the outcome."

"So, what do I do now?" Salena paced the small room, still rubbing her temples. She felt like her head was about to explode.

Heloise closed her eyes and shook her head. "The supernatural is unpredictable, but karma, either good or bad, will find a way. You will just have to wait and see how things play out, but I think the outcome will bring you love. I think you are on a journey to your soulmate," she stated with a wink.

Salena rolled her eyes in frustration. Love had always been a hassle for her, but what Heloise suggested was ridiculous. "Can't the cat I took in be enough?"

Devin listened intently to the tarot reading, and he was especially interested in the part regarding the past coming back to interfere. He must have been right about Gabriel's reason for being there. His brother had his eyes on Salena for a reason. That made Devin's muscles tense up and his fangs grind. He'd warned Gabriel to never come back again after what he'd tried to do to Abigail. He could still remember catching his brother with Abigail. She'd been trapped and defenseless underneath the vampire's body, struggling for her life when he'd walked in. Devin had yanked him off her just in time—if his fangs had broken her skin, she would've been marked as his to do with as he pleased. That was an understanding within the vampire race; it had been passed down by the eldest of them all. Apparently, though, Gabriel no longer cared about vampire etiquette.

The memory made his blood boil. He would not let Gabriel get close to Salena. He would protect her at all costs.

A black wolf ran faster than ever before, racing to catch up to Salena and, he assumed, Gabriel too.

Salena walked like someone in a trance up the porch steps and, after fumbling for the right key, into her house. After locking up, she went straight to her bed and curled up into a ball. It only took her a few minutes of soft sobs to fall asleep, and a terrifying dream took hold.

She was running through the woods with shadows chasing after her, and they were rapidly catching up. Snakes, bats, spiders, and wolves were all over the place. Everywhere she looked, there was darkness and shadows. An eerie howling filled the black air. She tried to run but ended up in a puddle of mud that was too thick to escape; her feet wouldn't budge. The shadows and creatures were right upon her, but all she could do was stand there—stuck—and scream.

Devin was watching Salena through her bedroom window while also trying to sense if Gabriel was nearby. He was out of practice, though, so he couldn't be sure. He watched her toss and turn; it appeared she was having a bad dream. Her beautiful mouth was in a deep frown, and her delicate eyebrows were stitched together.

Wanting to comfort his love, he shifted back into a black cat and entered through the old pet door. The door at the top of the steps still didn't have a lock. He slipped quietly into her kitchen and crept like a shadow down the hallway to her bedroom where he climbed into bed beside her and cradled his body against hers.

She began to stir at the motion, so he whispered into her ear, "somn de acum," *sleep for now*, to keep her deep in slumber. Then, to soothe away her bad dreams, he brushed his fingertips gently along her skin and ran them through her silky hair. As he stroked her, her breathing became slow and steady, and he could feel her racing heartbeat slow down as well. He placed a couple of soft kisses on her shoulder, and when he looked at her face, he was positive he saw a smile grace her lovely lips.

For the next half-hour, he just lay there holding her, caressing her, and washing over her with his love—not having any idea that they were both being watched.

Gabriel watched Devin and the woman through the window. It was sickening to watch Devin drool all over the mortal; albeit she was pretty. *Pretty enough to eat*, he thought wickedly. She was every bit as beautiful as Abigail was, but that was no reason to fall under the evil spell of a woman and risk the horrid possibility of becoming mortal again. Devin would never learn. Vampires were strong, while humans were weak, and strength always won out. If Gabriel couldn't stop Devin from becoming mortal again, he would just kill him afterward.

Watching the couple, he also found it disturbing that his brother could lay so close to a beautiful woman without using her body for his pleasure. Gabriel would rectify that mistake as soon as he got the chance, and his chance looked to be right then. Devin had gotten up, kissed her softly on the lips, and left out the front door.

Gabriel shifted into a brown owl and hid in the treetops—waiting.

Salena was having a peaceful and almost romantic dream. She had been stuck in terrifying black woods, trapped in mud, and hideous creatures were coming after her. There was also the shadow, which was probably the most terrifying part. Then, suddenly, a strong arm was around her waist, lifting her from the mud and pulling her into a protective embrace. She looked up to see the face of her savior, but it was too dark to distinguish his features.

Her protector whispered huskily in her ear, "It's okay. I've got you now, and you are safe with me."

She turned and saw the creatures and the shadow backing off. The entire scene changed; the woods were suddenly her bedroom, and her protector laid her softly onto her bed and climbed in with her. He held her tightly, caressed her, and whispered words of love. She turned to look at his face; however, just as she did, she woke up.

Salena felt frustrated for not getting to see the face of her hero before she woke up, but she was also relieved the nightmare part was over. Then she recalled her tarot reading earlier, and her living nightmare came flooding back to her along with anger. Knowing there had to be some mistake, or at least a further explanation, she got up from her nap and decided to head back to the voodoo shops to get one more reading. Hopefully, she would get a completely different one—maybe even a reading about the mystery man in her dream. She just hoped he wasn't a vampire.

The woman mesmerized Gabriel while she slept facing the window he was watching her through. The undistinguishable difference between her and Abigail took his breath away. Sure, he had recognized the similarities before, but they were even more striking as he watched her sleep. It was the perfect opportunity for him to make his move, but he just couldn't stop staring. He was transfixed by the raven beauty.

Suddenly, she woke up, grabbed her purse, and headed outside to her car. He followed her, deciding to play a game of chase.

48

Devin had left Salena's bed reluctantly, but he needed to hunt down his brother. He couldn't—no, he wouldn't—let Gabriel get ahold of her. He remembered perfectly well how sadistic his brother was. Well, he was more so than vampires were already considered to be. This was especially true when it came to a woman Devin loved.

He sniffed the air and thought he could pick up his brother's scent, but it wasn't strong enough to pinpoint his exact location. *He must be in animal form*, Devin worried. When vampires were shifted, their scent wasn't as strong. Devin quickly shifted into a black hawk, so he'd have keen eyesight and smell to track the other vampire.

Circling her house, he noticed that she was going somewhere. He got closer to the house and watched her leave, but at the same time, he caught Gabriel's scent. Unfortunately, by the time he realized where his brother had been perched, it was too late—the vampire was already gone and, no doubt, chasing Salena. Furious with himself, Devin blazed a trail after them.

How could I have let Gabriel get away unnoticed? He must have a new trick up his sleeve. Devin knew he had to end the vendetta before he became mortal—before it was too late.

Salena walked along the strip mall, which was filled with various clairvoyants and voodoo shops. She saw the one she'd visited before, but that reading hadn't gone too well, so she decided not to visit it again. She needed a fresh pair of eyes to look at her fate.

She noticed an elderly Gypsy woman, who was looking into a crystal ball, and before she could walk away, the Gypsy looked up at her with a secretive smile and a wink. Salena read the sign on the door—*Madame Marietta, Fortuneteller.* Again, she looked at the woman's kind face, and again, the woman gave her a wink.

Well, either she wants to date me, or she has something to tell me. Eager to get some good news and clarification, she stepped inside the shop.

"Welcome!" the robust Gypsy spoke louder than Salena expected, and it made her jump. "Do not be afraid, dear, I'm here to help you. Madame Marietta knows all."

What an original pitch. She started to explain to the woman, "Well, I'm here be—"

Madame Marietta cut her off, "I know why you are here. I saw it in my crystal ball. You have questions about the mysterious things going on in your life and the outcome of your future, which has much to do with the past."

Surprised at the Gypsy's accuracy, Salena could only nod. She felt more anxious—until this woman, she could still pretend that her tarot readings hadn't been real or at least not accurate. Slowly, though, her doubts were being washed away. *Oh crap*.

"I know you're scared because you don't yet comprehend the magical forces surrounding you; however, love comes in many different—sometimes unexpected— forms," the psychic explained.

Salena grumbled, "But I'm not in love, I'm not looking for love, and I'm not even dating."

Madame Marietta held up her hand, which was laden with colorful rings. "But love has found you, and from what I have seen, it is an epic love and by far more powerful than mortal love. This is why I wanted you to come in. Love like this shouldn't be and can't be ignored. It has come from the past to settle in you now, and the original recipient knows that. He knows where his lost love lies."

Agitated, Salena paced the room. "Why can't I meet a nice man and fall in love on my own terms like a normal person?"

Madame Marietta looked at her with soft eyes. "Because love chose you first. This enchantment started long ago with someone else close to you, and now it's back to finish what it started."

Salena looked at the Gypsy like she was crazy. "Close to me? If you are referring to Abigail, she was my tenth-generation great-grandmother, and that was almost three hundred years ago, so why is it after me? Why didn't one of my other relatives become his obsession?"

The psychic laughed lightly. "You are speaking of love like it's a disease instead of a gift. Truelove has a mind of its own. I cannot tell you why he chose you over someone else. I only see that he has, and you must not fight him. He is not going to let you go." Madame Marietta was smiling just as Heloise had.

"Well, then what can you tell me about *him*? What did you see?" Salena asked. She should at least have her questions about the vampire answered.

"I can tell you he has blood on his hands, but he only has love in his heart for you. He knows you have a connection to his past; again, he knows where his lost truelove lies. The supernatural realm exists beyond the reach of science and without complete proof, but that doesn't mean it isn't there. Look where you are, Salena. You are trusting me to tell you your future.

Completely stunned, Salena looked at the smiling woman. "I never told you my name."

"Oh, didn't you?" The Gypsy looked up from the crystal ball and winked.

"Okay, now I'm really scared. Why can't I just have a normal life? And if his love has 'settled' in me, as you say, why don't I feel it?"

"You have not yet opened up your mind and heart to it. Once you come to fully accept things the way they are, you will come to realize your destiny."

"What if I don't want this? What if I don't choose to accept the love of a vampire? Which I don't!" she ranted. Then, in a softer tone, she asked, "Do you think he's a vampire, too, or are you going to tell me something else?"

"Yes, he is a vampire. But he is a vampire in love, which is a rare thing. His heart calls to you like a mortal man's would."

"Well, his heart has the wrong number, so let it call someone else. Let him choose another's bloodline."

"I'm afraid, dear, the choice was made for him and for you as well. Love will always find its way. Just try to be open to it. It is a natural living thing, and I see that it is living in you now. You just haven't accepted it, yet."

"No, I don't accept that a blood-sucking vampire is my soulmate!" Salena threw her hands in the air. "This is crazy!"

"You haven't seen the complete picture yet. There is more to it than you think."

"So, give me answers then, please," she sighed.

"I see danger, but the one who seeks your heart is not the one who poses a threat to you. There is another who is also connected to the past. This source of pure evil will try to destroy you and your truelove. You must go to your lover and let him protect you and help you understand your destiny. You must trust him."

Salena paid for the reading and headed toward the door. "I can't take any more of this. No more bad news."

While getting into her car, she looked at her watch through teary eyes and saw that it was 6:00. It had already been such a long and terrible day. First, there was the funeral, then Heloise's tarot reading, and then this last one. She just wanted to go home and sleep peacefully.

Suddenly, she remembered she had plans. "Shit! Rob," she exclaimed to herself.

She'd forgotten about him, and she was supposed to meet him at 7:30 for dinner. That didn't give her enough time to politely cancel, so she headed home to change.

She chose to wear jeans with a blue tunic top and tennis shoes. Keeping with the casual theme, she topped off her outfit by pulling her long black hair into a ponytail.

50

While following Salena, Gabriel realized how hungry he was and how alone and tasty looking a cute brunette at the bus stop was. She must have been to the vampire tour because she was dressed in slutty Gothic clothes and wearing plastic fangs. She even had red bite marks penciled in on her throat. He laughed at the irony of the situation—she would soon have real ones.

He approached the young woman and licked his fangs in anticipation. As soon as she noticed him walking toward her, she thrust her chest out and flashed her dimples. Gabriel, like Devin, was impossible to resist. His six-foot-six frame was adorned with silky brown hair, which fell neatly to his broad shoulders, and his chiseled jaw was adorned with full luscious lips that were just begging to be kissed.

She noticed his mysterious black eyes, and tingles ran up and down her spine. He was so Goth and hot. She batted her lashes at him. "Hello. I like your costume. Did you go on the tour yet?" she asked with a demure smile.

Purely from amusement, he grinned back at the woman. "Hey there," he replied in a sensuous purr. "No, I haven't gone on a tour yet. Have you?" He flashed his full smile, including his fangs.

"Cool fangs! Where did you get those?"

He chuckled, "You wouldn't believe me if I told you. So, did you like the tour?"

"Yes, it was kind of cool," she responded, still admiring his teeth and body.

"Well, I might know of a better one. It's much more realistic," he told her while reaching for her hand. She had no way of knowing just how more realistic it was going to be.

"Really? Where at? I've not seen any others," she stated, noticing how warm and incredibly strong his hand was.

"Well, it's a private tour just for you," he replied while leading her away from the bus stop. "Care to check it out?" He flashed another big smile.

"Sure." In truth, she'd go anywhere with him.

Devin had caught up to Salena to make sure she was safe from Gabriel. He had, thankfully, discovered his brother's scent leading off in a different direction.

He was able to hear most of Salena's reading from Madame Marietta, and it pleased him to hear the fortuneteller explain to Salena how powerful his love was, and that it couldn't be ignored. Just as he was about to shapeshift to follow her, the door to Madame Marietta's shop opened.

"Wait! Don't go. I know who you are, and I need to speak to you. Please, come inside my shop."

The Gypsy motioned eagerly for him to follow her into the shop. Devin was curious, so he went with her. She locked the door behind him and pulled a thick curtain across the room. Then she reached out and grabbed his strong hand and led him behind it.

"I saw you in my crystal ball. You are in love with the woman who just left here—you are a vampire."

Devin was stunned. No one had ever approached him before while knowing what he was. "Why would you want me in here all alone with you?" he asked with an arched brow.

"Because I want your help," she replied in a serious tone. She sounded nervous, but she looked utterly determined about something.

"With what? What can a vampire help you with?" he wondered with a mixture of curiosity and amusement.

"As you can see, I'm getting along in years." She shrugged her shoulders and started wringing her hands while looking in his dark and mysterious eyes, pleading with her own. "And I am done. I don't want to wait for the ending I have foreseen. I want you to end it for me." She winked at him and tried to muster up a pleasing smile. "I can't think of a more pleasurable way to go than in the arms of a charming vampire like yourself." She cocked her head, exposing her neck for him. "Please, be gentle and quick."

Devin was bewildered. No one had ever asked to be bitten before. He brushed her cheek gently. "You have years left, my lady, so why would you ask this of me?"

"I am a psychic, and I can see glimpses of my future too. As I said, I don't want to go in the way I have foreseen—alone and in pain. Please, do this for me now because my day of reckoning is upon me. I beg you." She had a stream of tears rolling down from her shrewd eyes.

Devin felt compassion for the woman who was trying to bring Salena to him. "Okay," he relented.

Madame Marietta once again exposed her neck. He, however, gently scooped her into his arms, hugged her, and gave her a soft kiss on the lips before biting—as quickly and gently as possible—into her neck. She moaned softly but then smiled as he quickly suckled her life's blood. Soon, it was over.

Devin gently laid her lifeless body on the small sofa located in the back of the shop. Feeling remorseful for the woman, he flipped her closed sign over and left, locking the door behind him.

It was time to find Salena, so he shifted into a black crow and hurried to find her before her date. The intrusive man she was meeting had no idea what was about to come down on him.

He quickly flew toward her home while keeping a vigilant eye out for Gabriel.

Gabriel appeased his next meal by letting her lead him down the sidewalk while holding his hand. She smirked at the envious women staring at her, and it gave him smug satisfaction.

Other women always judged Tina for being into Goth, so she loved watching them be jealous of her with the gorgeous stranger. She was willing to bet none of their men looked as good. Just to rub the salt in more, she stopped, stood on her tiptoes, and kissed him long and hard, tracing his fangs with the tip of her tongue.

The young woman's forwardness amused Gabriel, but he obliged her. He even started to get aroused. In fact, he was sure she could feel his erection pressed against her abdomen because it made her kiss him deeper and harder.

Tina grabbed the sexy stranger's hand again and hurried him around the block and into the rundown apartment she lived in with two other women. They would be gone for at least another hour, which was plenty of time for her to get what she wanted from the handsome man—his body.

Gabriel mumbled, "Okay, I guess we're going to your place." She was making it too easy for him.

She locked the door behind him and immediately grabbed his growing erection with one hand while running the other up his flat abs to reach around his neck. She pulled herself up for another long kiss and began to nibble on his lips and tongue.

He almost laughed at her aggressiveness. "So, you like to bite, huh?"

"Yes," came her breathless reply as she started to bite his neck—gently at first, then harder.

Gabriel, getting hungrier and thicker, opened her jeans and yanked them down. He wasn't surprised that she had on a black thong, which he ripped off in one swift movement. She'd already opened his black pants and was stroking him hard and fast. He moved her hand away, though, and asked, "Hey, what's your name, pretty girl?"

While stroking the head of his throbbing girth, she answered, "Tina. Why?"

He lifted her off the ground and thrust hard inside her. Then he answered with a menacing growl, "Because I want to know who *I'm* going to bite." He ripped into her throat with five days' worth of thirst.

53

Salena pulled up in front of The Edgar Degas House at 7:35. She immediately spotted Rob, who was waiting in his car, but she didn't notice the black crow that was also waiting.

Rob got out of his car and opened his passenger door for her. "Hi, Salena. I'm glad you took me up on my offer, and thanks for not standing me up."

"Hi, Rob. I'm sorry that I'm late," she mumbled.

She looked at him and then scowled when she turned her head away. Rob just wasn't her type. She thought wistfully of Eric and the other day with him, and then she thought about her mysterious vampire lover. Either way, Rob paled in comparison.

"It's okay. I'm just glad you showed up. What do you feel like eating?" he asked and glanced at her with a kind smile.

She replied, "How about Chinese? I haven't had that lately."

"Sure, that sounds good to me." He quickly drove toward the Moon Wok, asking her questions about her job along the way.

Enjoy her company while you still can, Devin thought sadistically and followed them to the restaurant.

Rob and Salena were seated right away next to a huge fish tank, and Salena wondered if any of the fish were intended to be someone's dinner. She didn't care for fish, so she decided to order pork.

"So, are you feeling better?" Rob asked with an uneasy smile. "I know how upset you are about Jane. She talked about you all the time, so I figured you guys were close."

With all that had happened after the funeral earlier, Salena hadn't thought much about Jane since. She didn't want to talk about her best friend with a stranger either, and fresh tears filled her eyes.

"Sorry for getting weepy, but it's been a terrible day. I just hope they catch the guy responsible."

She left it at that. She wasn't about to tell him about the other crazy things going on. The waitress had dropped off their drinks and two fortune cookies before taking their order. Salena was glad for the interruption to the uncomfortable conversation. Again, she wished she hadn't accepted his invite.

"Yeah, me too. Shall we see what our fortunes are?" Rob looked at her with childlike enthusiasm.

Salena mumbled to herself, "I've already seen it, and it sucks."

"What?" Rob asked and raised his eyebrows.

"Nothing." Out of curiosity, she opened her cookie. *Keep your eyes open to all possibilities.* She crumpled the slip of paper up and put it with her straw wrapper.

Rob didn't look happy about his either. He read it aloud, "Trouble is heading your way." He shrugged it off. "Whatever."

"Mine was dumb too," Salena declared.

She looked around the restaurant, trying to avoid conversation and eye contact. Why did she agree to go out with him? And more importantly, how could she get out of it early? Just as she was thinking of a headache excuse, she saw their food coming. It figured she would pick a restaurant with fast service.

Devin, hidden among the other patrons, heard Rob's fortune and couldn't agree more. Trouble was definitely heading the man's way. He was glad to see that Salena wasn't having a good time on her date, and he wished he could help her end it early. She should be with *him*, preferably in her bed.

"So, how long have you known Jane?" Rob inquired.

Salena put her fingertips to her temples. "I can't talk about her, Rob. It's just been too soon, and I'm not ready. It's just too hard to talk about. Can we actually just go? I'm sorry, but I'm getting a migraine."

"Oh, I'm sorry to hear that. Let me get the check." Rob stood up to find their waitress. There was an obvious look of disappointment on his face.

Salena felt bad for hurting his feelings; she could tell he was interested in her. She decided to tell him that she just wanted to be friends, so she wasn't leading him on. Then she wondered again if he might be the one getting into her house. But that was absurd. *Rob isn't a vampire, is he? He isn't big enough, or attractive enough for that matter, to be the man from the phone booth.* The thought made her feel confused, terrified, and utterly helpless. So did believing in vampires.

Rob returned to the table and pulled her chair out for her. He'd brought her a container to wrap up her uneaten food, and while she scraped the meal into it, he pulled a white daisy out of his pocket.

"I meant to give this to you earlier," he told her sheepishly. "I heard you like daisies."

"Thank you," she responded while getting up from the table. "I think I have a new cat who will like this dinner." She didn't dare tell him about her new *boyfriend*.

Rob put his arm around her waist to escort her from the restaurant, but she pulled away from his hold. Just as he was about to reach for her hand, he was sure he heard a low growl from somewhere close by, so he looked over his shoulder, but he didn't see anyone looking at them.

He had the feeling that they were being followed out to the parking lot, too, but when he looked around, he didn't see anyone else.

As they walked toward his car, he exclaimed, "Wow, it's really nice out tonight. Would you like to take a short walk?"

Salena considered the offer. She supposed the fresh air might actually do her some good, so she answered, "Sure, as long as it's quick. My migraine medicine is at home."

Once again, Rob put his arm around her waist, and once again, she pulled away. He was getting angry, thinking she shouldn't be so distant to him. He reached for her hand and took a firm hold on it. It felt cold and clammy, which he chalked up to nerves about the goodnight kiss. Again, he thought he heard a low growl somewhere close by. In fact, he was certain of it, and he couldn't stop from shuddering. Salena must've heard it, too, because she looked around them.

Salena wished he would stop touching her. She didn't want to lead him on, and she had no intentions of going out with him again. She also wished whatever she heard growl would head in a different direction. Spotting a bench nearby, she decided it was a good time to break the news to Rob. She pointed it out, and he agreed to go sit with her.

Salena sat down first, but then he sat so close to her, she had to scoot away, and it appeared to make him mad. She began, "Rob, I think you expect more from me than I am willing to give. I have too much going on in my life to think about a relationship right now." Then, after seeing a hopeful look still lingering on his face, she added, "Or to even think about dating. I would like to be friends, though."

"Oh, I see. I really like you, so that's a shame." He started to reach for her hand one more time, as a last effort, but she quickly pulled away, and then he was sure he heard a deep and terrifying growl from somewhere behind them. "Did you hear that? Is that a dog?"

Salena looked around, too, and softly replied, "I'm not sure, but if it is, it's a big one."

"Well, either way, I think we should go, don't you?" His voice was quivering.

She nodded, and he led the way back to his car at a pace that she found difficult to keep up with. She didn't complain, though. She was ready to get far away from the growling noise.

They reached his car in record time, and he was quiet all the way back to The Edgar Degas House. She was glad to avoid uncomfortable conversation, but the silence was awkward too. She wondered how angry he was with her, and when he pulled up by her car, she got her answer. Rob turned into a different person—one she didn't expect and one she didn't like.

"Why the hell did you agree to go out with me if you didn't want to date me?" he gruffly demanded.

Startled, she backed up from him. "I'm sorry, Rob. I didn't mean to hurt you."

"You led me on!" he screeched.

Then, shocking her even further, he grabbed her and pressed his mouth to hers with painful force while grabbing her breasts with even more gusto.

"Stop it!" Salena struggled and tried to scream, but the sound was lost in his disgusting mouth. She could hear her top ripping, and her flesh was burning from his roaming, squeezing hands.

"You even dressed like a slut for me tonight. I know you want me."

"I did not! You're crazy!" she screamed just as he was forcing her jeans open against her struggling hands and her attempts to punch him. "Stop it!"

For a slender man, he was surprisingly strong. He slapped her and pushed her into his back seat. Then he tried to climb on top of her in the small space. She could feel her nose bleeding, and she could feel his erection pressing against her, which brought on a wave of nausea.

Just as he was undoing his pants, there was a loud sound of steel grinding against steel and a rush of air. Suddenly, the weight of Rob was gone. Not caring how, Salena clutched her torn top around her exposed breasts, grabbed her purse, and fled. Once inside her car, she sped down Esplanade Avenue like her life depended on it—and she was fairly certain it did.

54

Rob had no idea what was happening to him. One minute, he was showing that tease, Salena, he had every intention of being more than her "friend," and the next minute, he felt like a train was running him over. He heard the crunching of steel and then felt his limbs being ripped out of their sockets as he was flying through the air. He had no time to respond to the searing, fiery pain torturing his body. He screamed in harmony with the sound of vicious growling and snarling. His bones were crushed, ligaments were torn, flesh was ripped, and his blood spilled out. He couldn't see who or what was attacking him through his tear-soaked eyes. He only knew his life was over, but he had no idea why. Finally, with one more torrid laceration, the torment ended and brought about the peaceful blackness of death.

Devin, still furious and covered in blood, shifted into a hawk and flew as fast as he could after Salena, who made it difficult for him to catch up. He hoped Gabriel would show up later, so he could bring down his blazing wrath upon him as well. He almost got his chance.

Gabriel had finally found Salena again. He'd been amused to see that she was dating a mortal instead of succumbing to his brother's charms. *Devin must not be at the top of his game anymore.* It was even more amusing when he watched the puny mortal man accost her. Then Devin had to show up and ruin it just as Gabriel was starting to have respect for the mortal.

He stayed to watch the punishment inflicted by Devin, which was unequivocally gruesome—just the way Gabriel liked it. He also watched Salena rush off. It was too bad, he thought, that the man didn't get to finish what he'd started—maybe he should track her down and finish it himself. The wicked thought made Gabriel's lip curl up. Then again, a confrontation with Devin at the moment might not be wise. It would be in his best interest to try to surprise his brother when he wasn't already enraged. Instead, he'd go scrounge up some entertainment and dinner. Sniffing the air, he found out he needn't travel far— he headed to a nearby park.

There was a young blond sitting on the park bench, and she was playing around on her smart phone. "Good evening," he greeted her, flashing a smile.

Looking up at the gorgeous man, trying to see him in the light from the lamppost, she instantly smiled back. "Good evening to you too." Then she shyly looked away and went back to her phone.

Gabriel sat down next to her and made small talk before dining on her. He didn't have time for sex, even though she was an easy target. He had to go check on Salena. She was, after all, the prize.

55

Salena ran up the stairs and unlocked her door with trembling hands. She couldn't help but keep looking over her shoulder to make sure she wasn't followed. What had gotten into Rob and, while utterly thankful he was gone, where did he go?

Inside the house, she locked the door and pushed her armchair against it. Her wrist was already hurting from fighting against Rob's attack, so moving furniture wasn't a big help for the pain, but she'd do whatever it took to keep the maniac out.

Of course, what about keeping a vampire out? How do you do that? Apparently, there wasn't a way; nonetheless, she ran through the house checking all the windows and doors. They were, of course, locked except the upstairs basement door. She really needed to get that fixed, not that one more lock in an already locked home would keep him out. It suddenly occurred to her that perhaps the vampire was getting in through the pet door. *No, he was too large to be able to do that,* she told herself.

Still, grabbing the largest kitchen knife she could find, she headed slowly and softly down the steps—really wishing they didn't creak. The single light she had flipped on at the top of the stairs only dimly lit the musty basement. Until the other day with Officer Marx, Salena hadn't gone down there since January, and that was just to put Christmas decorations away. She had always thought basements were creepy, which is why she insisted on a house with an upstairs laundry room. As quickly as possible, she checked the locks on the patio door and windows, which were all intact, leaving only the pet door. She looked at the small door, still wondering, and then pushed a heavy crate in front of it. It would have to do until she could board it up. As she climbed back up the stairs, she had the eerie feeling of being watched. She looked behind her but couldn't see anyone outside the windows or door. Brushing it off as nerves, she stepped into the kitchen and grabbed a chair to prop up under the basement door handle. She wasn't taking any chances. Then, desperately needing to unwind, she made some chamomile tea and drew a candlelight bubble bath—it was the perfect way to relax.

She grabbed her phone to call the police about Rob but then decided she'd wait a day. He did run off after coming to his senses. Maybe he was just grief stricken over Jane, and her rejection was more than he could handle. She'd wait to see if he apologized, but she would never go anywhere with him again. That was for certain.

Devin watched Salena nervously biting her nails and checking her locked doors and windows. He felt hurt because he knew she was trying to keep him out when all he wanted to do was kiss her fears away and tell her everything was going to be all right.

He almost wished she'd seen the punishment exacted on the man to put her mind at ease. She'll find out justice was done soon enough, but would she know he was the one who saved her, and that he did it out of love?

He was surprised when she'd blocked the pet door, but it wouldn't be a problem. There was always a way in. Shifted into a black crow, he was perched on her windowsill watching her take a bath. Her body was so beautiful, silhouetted by the candlelight. It shadowed her in a mysterious way, but at the same time, it gave Devin a good enough peek at her body to make his blood burn with desire. His wings started flapping and hit the window, making her jump up in the tub.

Salena wasn't sure what was outside her window, but she wasn't going to wait to find out. She grabbed her towel and quickly blew out the candles.

Once inside her bedroom, she locked the door behind her and dressed as quickly as possible. Then she hid underneath the covers. *Like that would really help.* She lay there shivering from her fear and thought about Eric. She wished he was there to protect her. She'd always felt safe with him around. But could he even protect her from a vampire?

When her cell phone rang from the nightstand, she jumped out of the covers and her skin. It was Heloise. "Hello?" she answered, nervous about what the woman had to say.

"Salena, I had a vision of you in trouble. Are you okay?" There was deep concern in her voice.

Salena sniffled and wailed, "I'm not sure what happened, and I'm really scared! One minute this guy, Rob, was going to rape me, and then suddenly he was gone, so

I left as fast as I could. And just now, there was something outside my bathroom window. What is going on?"

Heloise replied calmly, "I'm not sure. I saw you in a pool of darkness, but then there was a light, and I could see the light covering the darkness. Then there was nothing. I was hoping to hear that your truelove saved you from the blackness." Her voice held a hopeful tone.

Salena groaned—enough with the truelove nonsense. "I don't know what happened. He was just gone all of a sudden, and I didn't care how. I got the hell out of there and didn't look back!"

"I think your soulmate rescued you," Heloise replied in a soothing tone. "You must allow yourself to yield to him and your destiny. You saw it in the cards, Salena. You can't deny what is meant to be. Love is going to find its way."

"No, you saw it, and Madame Marietta saw it, and Madame Zoyla did too, while the voodoo priestess at Marie Laveau's House of Voodoo saw danger. I just see a bunch of nonsense meant to scare people. Rob is a human being—not a vampire or some fictitious monster. Or at least I didn't think he was a monster." She was almost shouting at the woman.

"There is still that shadow to reckon with, Salena. That is the danger the priestess warned you about, but you must trust your truelove to protect you from it. That's what my vision says to me—at all cost, he will protect you. It's like I told you earlier. There is another here from the past to stop you and your truelove."

"A vampire will protect me? From what, his relative?" Salena was shouting into the phone. She sounded much like a stubborn child, who was throwing a tantrum. She was embarrassed by her own behavior, but everyone had to admit—believers or not—it was all ridiculous. "The police said the DNA was a familial match," she added in a softer tone.

"Well, I suppose that could be true. Your love can explain it all to you. Before I go, just know that all will be revealed soon, my dear. Take heart that you are safe when your love is near. He'll save you." The phone clicked, and the line went dead.

Salena set the phone back down and lay in her bed, trying to close her eyes, but she was too nervous. She'd left her bedside lamp on, and there was no way she was turning it off. She kept looking around the room—in the corners, at the curtained window, at her locked bedroom door, and at the closet door, which she'd tied shut with a scarf. Finally, her eyes got too heavy, and she drifted off.

Devin's heart broke for the terrified woman, and he wished he could hold her. He wished that she was ready to accept him and their love. He stood outside her window, and to help her fall asleep, he whispered, "Somn profund acum." *Slumber deeply now.* Then he blew her a kiss. Once he heard the soft sound of her snoring, he went to the pet door, reached in and pushed the crate out of his way, and then shifted into a black cat to slip inside.

Her bedroom door was still locked, so he shifted into a black spider to crawl underneath it. Once inside the bedroom, he knelt before her and whispered, "Doar visezi." *You are just dreaming.* Then he kissed her softly with his tongue delving deeply into her mouth. He expertly probed every corner and fed on her sweetness.

Her eyes fluttered opened, and thinking she was just dreaming, she fully responded to his delicious kiss with a voracious invitation. Her response instantly made his shaft grow thicker and harder, and a low growl escaped from his throat. She moaned softly in response—yes, she was under his spell.

She put her hands around his neck and traced his massive shoulders. They were so magnificently broad, and his biceps were enormous. She broke away from his kiss to study his face in the lamplight. He was shockingly handsome with long black hair, black eyes to match, full and sensuous lips, and a masculine jaw adorned with a very sexy chin cleft, which she traced with her slender fingertip.

Her behavior must have turned him on because he growled again, and taking her hands in his, he pulled her out of her bed to stand before him.

"Good Lord you're tall," she gasped.

With a low chuckle, he put one hand on the small of her back to pull her closer, while the other ran through her hair and along her delicate features. Then he claimed her mouth once again. He kissed her with a fierce passion that produced a deep smoldering heat between her slender thighs. She pressed her breasts against his broad, brawny chest and urged his already roaming hands to continue their blazing path down her form.

She breathed into his mouth, "Take me."

Elated and more aroused than he had been since Abigail, Devin scooped her up and carried her back to the inviting bed. Salena was already trying to get his shirt open, so he lent her a hand and ripped it off. She planted heated kisses on his splendid chest while he was ripping her nightgown open. He laid her down and gently placed himself on top of her. He braced his weight on his left arm while his right hand was gently caressing her beautiful, voluptuous breasts. Feeling like his pants were about to split open, he groaned and took a taut rosy peak into his mouth and suckled with fervent hunger.

She squirmed in response and grabbed handfuls of his hair before raking her nails down his chest and clutching at his full, throbbing male heat. She moaned in pleasure from his mouth teasing her sensitive bud, but also from the size of his masculinity, straining to get out of his pants.

Trying to unfasten the pants, she huskily told him, "I want you inside me now."

He chuckled, both amused and stimulated by her eagerness to make love. "Uh-uh." He stopped her hands and pinned her wrists above her head. "I'm not done pleasuring you and working you up for me yet. I want to taste you."

He ripped his pants off, finally freeing his hot, bulging flesh. As her eyes widened and pooled with lust at the sight of his exposed pulsating manhood, he moved down her slender body, trailing it with the tip of his tongue, making her moan from need—she was already enjoying herself, but it was about to get a lot more intense for her. He traced the fingertips of his right hand up the insides of her left thigh and grazed them over her aching mound and swollen, petal-soft lips.

She put her hands on top of his, urging him on and trying to force his hand deeper into her cleft, but he stopped her and chuckled again.

"Not yet, my love. You need to have patience," he purred.

Then to torment her further, he rose back over her body and used the tip of his tongue to trace little circles on her pink aching bud. Then he blazed a path down her abdomen and settled between her satiny folds. He lapped at the nectar waiting there for him and ran the tip of his tongue all around her velvety softness before taking her into his mouth.

Salena felt herself explode into a thousand shards of light from the expertise of his ravenous mouth. "Take me!" she screamed again.

Thinking his feisty vixen needed release as much as he did, he rose above her and slid inside her welcoming body. Her tight center almost caused him to lose control. He had to keep thrusting and withdrawing until her stretching walls engulfed him.

Salena was moaning and writhing in exquisite, torturous pleasure. He was so masculine—her dream lover—and she begged herself, *please don't wake up*. Her climaxes came in splendid undulations, and she didn't want it to end. She grabbed his perfect, firm ass and dug her nails into his taut skin to urge him to keep going.

Devin was riding her waves of pleasure, and as her body convulsed around him, he thrust deeper and harder to make their mutual pleasure more intense. As his own sweet shuddering moment approached, he moved his mouth from her nipple, where he'd been teasing her some more, to the soft inside of her perfect mound and gently bit.

She squealed from the nip and looked into his black eyes. "You," was all she could mutter under the flames and tides of passion consuming her.

"Yes," he replied in a ravenous growl. While he licked up her sweet blood, he ruptured inside her slick heat. The taste was so good, so perfect, and it astounded him. If he'd had any doubts about her being Abigail's great-granddaughter before, he didn't any longer.

While his body still shivered from his explosive climax, he hugged her tightly, lovingly, and protectively—as if both their lives depended on it—and with Gabriel somewhere close by, it did.

57

Gabriel watched the lovers from a corner in Salena's bedroom. Devin wasn't the only one who had snuck in under the locked door. Gabriel stayed shifted into a tiny brown recluse, so Devin wouldn't be able to sense him. Catching up to them was more appealing to him than going into town to feed again. If he got lucky, he'd just feed on her. He could definitely understand his brother's attraction to Abigail's mirror image. She was stunning, and she also looked like she was great in bed. He'd have to sample her for himself as soon as Devin slunk away.

He was getting bored sitting on the windowsill and watching Devin caress her naked body. He wondered how his brother would react if he really knew what had happened to Abigail. What if he knew that Gabriel was the one to cry *witch*? And how would he feel if Gabriel could take away his love and key to mortality again? Oh, yes, coming back to the U.S. was an excellent decision.

In what seemed liked hours, Devin finally left. Gabriel waited until his brother's presence could no longer be sensed before he approached Salena's sleeping form. No doubt Devin needed to find prey, or perhaps, he was out looking for him. The latter thought was amusing.

He crawled down from his post and was just about to shapeshift into human form when he sensed Devin was back. *Damn the luck*. Apparently, he didn't go too far. Oh well, it didn't matter because he would still take a taste. The brown recluse climbed up the bedpost and used all of his eyes to take in the sight of her gorgeous naked body before crawling onto her neck and sinking his spider fangs in. Her blood was invigorating. It was the sweetest and warmest he'd ever tasted, and he filled up on it. The venom from his bite wouldn't hurt her much, but it would, hopefully, let Devin know he'd been there. Then, since he couldn't have his way with her, he crawled back under the door and left the house on the opposite side of where Devin was perched, watching her sleep. Hungry, Gabriel went in search of prey.

He hoped Devin would catch enough of his scent to know he'd not protected his woman—again.

Devin hadn't wanted to leave Salena's side, especially after their passionate lovemaking, but he'd needed to check for Gabriel's whereabouts; unfortunately, he'd had no luck in finding him. Then after watching her sleep for a few hours, he realized how badly he needed to feed. It'd been a couple of days since he'd fed, not counting the low estrogen Madame Marietta. Her blood hadn't really done anything for him, and it certainly wasn't enough to hold him over. He needed the blood of a young woman; therefore, back in human form, he strolled into town to see what was on the menu.

As soon as he approached a local nightclub on Main Street, he caught the eyes of several ladies. Some, he could tell, were looking for customers, while the others were just looking for fun. He had his pick of many different shapes, colors, and sizes to choose from. He'd already picked out a young blond, who looked to be in her twenties, and he was approaching her when a working girl walked up to him. The woman appeared nervous and gave him a weak pick up line.

"Are you looking for a good time, gorgeous?" She tried to pose in a sexy manner but lost her balance on her five-inch heels and fell into him.

Helping her regain her balance, he told her, "I'll have to pass tonight. I'm just looking for dinner." He brushed her hair out of her overly-made-up face and added, "It's your lucky night." There was just something too pitiful about the woman to even bother with her. So, he stepped aside and went after the blond instead.

The blond saw him approaching and gave him a flirty smile. She was dressed in a flimsy tank top and Daisy Duke shorts, showing off long, tanned legs.

"Good evening. What's a pretty girl like you doing here without a man?" he asked, flashing a seductive smile even though he didn't intend to seduce her. She was only about sustenance—he needed to be strong for Salena, to help her understand their destiny, and he needed to be strong to fight off his brother.

The blond looked up at him, batting her lashes. "I'm here waiting for you." She reached out and patted his chest playfully. "It's a beautiful night, so would you care to take a walk with me?"

Devin proffered his arm to her, and she eagerly accepted. He led her down the street to the bus stop where there was some privacy. "Would you like to sit down and talk?" He gestured gallantly to the bench.

"Sure." She plopped down, making her breasts bounce. "What's your name?"

Devin sat close to her and replied, "My name is Devin. What's yours?"

"I'm Amber, and it's nice to meet you, Devin." She held out her hand to shake, but he took it and kissed it instead. She giggled, "Well, aren't you the old-fashioned gentleman?" Then she leaned into him and asked, "Do you want to kiss me?"

Devin avoided her mouth, though, and went for her throat instead and just planted kisses there—for the moment. Her pulse quickened under his lips, and even though a couple of people were standing nearby, he whispered, "No," and sank his fangs into her.

"Oh!" Amber yelped at the puncture, but then she smiled and moaned—possibly assuming he was giving her a hickey.

It was over with quickly, and he left her body propped up on the bench with her glassy eyes staring out at absolutely nothing.

Devin suddenly caught Gabriel's scent and moved away from the bus stop and dead girl. His brother was close—close enough to kill, perhaps. He followed the scent for two blocks to an abandoned storefront where he discovered the prostitute who'd tried to solicit him earlier dead. Not that he needed to, he turned the woman's head to the side, and there it was—Gabriel's bite mark. He felt sorry for the woman again. He'd turned her away because he'd thought she was pitiful, and now she truly was.

Knowing he had to get back to Salena as soon as possible, he shifted into a black hawk and flew as fast as his wings would allow him. If he was too late, he'd bring the fires of hell down on the whole damn city. He'd turn it over, top to bottom, until he found his brother.

59

Salena woke up from the most erotic dream of
her life. Her body was still shuddering from it. Then she
looked down at her naked body, and she was livid. He'd
done it again! He'd been there and seduced her again. *Is this
what love with a vampire is like—supernatural date rape?* It would
figure that the best sex of her life was while she was under
a vampire's spell. It had been amazing; there was no
denying that. Still, he had no right to trick her, and it wasn't
the way to win her love, not that she ever intended to give
it to him.

Angry and wide-awake, she clicked on the TV in
her bedroom while she got dressed. It was almost 7:00 a.m.
and time for the morning news. She was not at all prepared,
though, to see what was in the headline. The newscaster
reported the increasing number of victims found with
peculiar bite marks on them. Then, when the cameras went
live at various locations, Salena saw Clive and some of the
locals in the background at one of the vampire tours. They
were shouting and holding up signs. *Do you believe now?* was

printed on a few signs. Salena closed her eyes, feeling angry and nauseated. *Yes, I believe now.* Was this the work of her alleged truelove? How could she ever possibly love a monster? How could Abigail have loved him?

She was going to fight this tooth—or fang in her case—and nail. She refused to accept her fate as the mistress of a vampire. Then she considered the possibility that it was the other vampire she'd seen creating the mayhem. What was the familial connection between the two of them, and should she assume there are more vampires roaming the streets of New Orleans? She paced her bedroom, nervously biting her nails again. The vampire definitely owed her a manicure.

She was pulled out of her thoughts when a photo of Rob graced the screen, and she turned up the volume. The reporter talked of another grisly murder involving the man in the photograph, accountant Rob Miller, whose body was found last night. He had crushed bones, torn ligaments, gashes, and a significant amount of blood loss. Police theorized that he might have been the victim of a hit-and-run, but nothing would be confirmed until an autopsy was performed, and the crime scene was fully processed. Salena thought again of how Rob had suddenly vanished from the car. She wondered if he ran off, after realizing his actions, and got hit by a truck.

But that doesn't explain Heloise's vision of darkness and then a light. What in the world is going on? Salena ran to her bathroom and retched.

Hands still shaking, she turned off the TV and went into the kitchen to fix some toast and chamomile tea to calm her nerves and settle her stomach. They helped until she turned the TV back on. There was a picture of Madame Marietta on the screen, and the reporter stated that her janitor found her body inside her shop late last night. Madame Marietta only had a bite mark on her neck, which was similar to the bite marks on the other female victims recently found, but no sexual activity was evident. The news crew was reporting live from the shop, and Salena saw the voodoo priestess in the background. She was holding up totems and a voodoo doll.

Salena cried softly for the woman whom she barely knew. Then she felt rage. Why would he hurt that Gypsy? She was old and kind, and she even rooted for him! How could she possibly be expected to swoon over a vicious killer? She got up and paced her kitchen while biting her nails again. Then she heard her cell phone ringing in the bedroom. *Who could be calling this early?* Maybe it was Heloise again. What if she had another vision? Salena ran to get the phone.

It was Eric. He told her he was back from London and was in town for business and wanted to check up on her. He invited her to dinner, and she accepted with reluctance. She would be glad to see him, but she was mad that he was conveniently late for the funeral, when she'd really needed him. Also, last night with Rob wouldn't have happened if Eric had been there.

Feeling a desperate need to clear her head, Salena went to the local lake to relax and contemplate her situation. So much had happened in the course of one week—her vacation week—and she thought she might lose her mind. There were vampires, murdered friends, reincarnation and soulmate theories, attempted rape, and an old boyfriend—how much could one person survive?

In the middle of her misery, she noticed a sting in her neck and got out her compact mirror to check the spot.

There was a bite mark; however, it wasn't like the other bite marks she'd had recently—the *vampire* bite marks she'd had recently. This one was more like a blister and was painful. She had already been nauseous, which she attributed to the upsetting morning news, but now she thought it might be something else. A trip to the doctor would be wise under normal circumstances, but nothing was normal about her life anymore, so she decided to go home and check it out online first. She couldn't dare cry "vampire" in public, not even in New Orleans.

Salena felt utterly foolish researching vampire bite marks while examining the mark in a handheld mirror. Nothing quite matched, so she typed in the description and found, oddly enough, images for spider bites that closely matched. She was really expecting it to be vampire related. She laughed at herself. Was she just losing her sanity? Then she remembered being bitten during her amazing dream and looked down at her breast. Lifting her left breast up in the bra cup, she saw the bite mark on the underside. No, unfortunately, she was perfectly sane, even though the entire situation was full of lunacy.

She looked back at the computer screen and saw that the bite on her neck was most likely that of a brown recluse. Since they are poisonous, she carefully followed the treatment advice listed. She thoroughly cleansed with anti-bacterial soap and then put a cold compress on it to reduce swelling and stop the spread of venom. She followed with some antibiotic ointment. There wasn't anything else to do but keep an eye on it.

Salena felt miserable, scared, and she missed Jane. Jane was the only friend she could confide in, not that she was sure how she would've brought this up to her. Karen had been more of a friend by association to Jane, and there was no way she would involve Eric. The only person she could really discuss it with was Heloise, and she was pro vampire. In fact, the other gypsies were all for it too. *Is there a conspiracy among the supernatural?* Thinking these crazy thoughts made her feel more out of touch with reality than she already felt, and given the absurdity of it all, she supposed the person she should confide in is a shrink.

Salena met Eric at the Red Fish Grill at 8:00 for a late dinner. She didn't want him to come to the house first because she knew she wouldn't be able to resist him, just like the last time, and then she'd feel foolish and used, just like the last time. If she ever wanted to move on with her life, she had to cut the ties with him. This had to be their last "goodbye." She wasn't going to agree to see him anymore after this evening. She couldn't just be friends with benefits, and she couldn't live her life on his terms either, not that she was even sure he still wanted her to.

He was already at the restaurant and gave her a kiss on the cheek. "Salena," he began after their drink order was placed, "I need to apologize. I shouldn't have made love to you the other night. It was just so familiar being back in that house with you again, and even with you splattered in paint."

"Yeah, it was familiar for me too," she agreed and started to feel flushed from the memory of it.

"But it was a mistake. I shouldn't have done that. I'm engaged, Salena."

It was like throwing a bucket of ice on her. "What?" she shrieked, causing many heads to turn in their direction. "Why the hell did you even call me then? Apparently, you've gotten over us already, but it still hurts for me!" She could feel the tears welling up, but she didn't look away.

"I know, and I called you because I wanted to tell you in person about her, but when I saw you, everything came flooding back. It hurt me, too, when we broke up. I really did want to have a life together, but I was done here"—he gestured openly—"I was done in New Orleans." His eyes stared deeply into hers, pleading for forgiveness.

Salena blotted at her tears with her cloth napkin and looked up at his humbled expression. She was prepared to give him a very big piece of her mind, but the power unexpectedly went out. It wasn't just the restaurant either, it was everywhere. The entire block was completely black.

The loud sounds of crashing dishes and anxious customers filled the restaurant, while blaring car horns and squealing tires filled the night air. Salena sat completely still, afraid to move as she felt people bumping into her.

"Eric?" she called out in the dark but received no answer.

Suddenly, warm, strong hands cupped her face. They were followed by lips on hers that were soft but strong, warm, comforting, and inviting. *How could he put the move on me again after what he just told me? How could I let him?* Because she loved him—still. She accepted the kiss and reached up to run her hands through his short, thick blond hair. But what she felt wasn't Eric's hair—it was long hair. She tried to break off the kiss to scream, but the lips and hands were suddenly gone. Then she realized something—it wasn't Eric's musk she was smelling either.

The lights came back on, showing food and broken dishes everywhere and an empty seat across from Salena. Just like that, he'd abandoned her without a word. *Unless he didn't have a choice...*

Salena quickly left the restaurant. She didn't want to be sitting there if Eric came back, and she certainly didn't want to be sitting there if the other person came back. *Person? Nope, vampire.* She thought about the long hair her hands had run through. It was the same long hair in her dream. Or, at least, what she'd thought was a dream at the time.

She rushed inside her house and locked the door. Her cell phone rang, startling her, and she assumed it was Eric—but it wasn't.

"Salena, leave your house immediately!" Heloise commanded her. "There's no time to explain; just get out of there now and come straight here. Hurry! Go!" then the line was dead.

Scared witless, Salena grabbed her purse and ran back to her Ford Focus. But just as she opened the car door, a brown owl dove at her with its talons out. It managed to grab a chunk of her hair and scratch her scalp while she flung her arms wildly. Finally, she managed to get into her car, and she slammed the door shut, catching the tip of one of the owl's wings. The bird flapped crazily while she was backing up until it finally freed itself from its prison.

Salena felt blood in her hair from the scratch, and while she was frightened by the bird's attack, she had no idea how lucky she was to leave when she did.

61

"Damn!" Gabriel cursed himself for stopping off for a snack on the way to Salena's house. The hooker didn't even taste good. Rubbing his arm now, injured from the car door, he cursed into the night air, "Bitch! This isn't over." And it wasn't. He'd get even with her—he'd break both of her arms before he finished her off.

He decided to vent his anger on her tidy little house. He burst through the front door and smashed everything in sight. He broke antiques and priceless mementos, and he ripped into the material on her furniture. Then, for his brother's sake, he went into her bedroom and marked his territory by urinating around her bed. Before he could continue on his path of destruction, though, he was stopped. His keen sense of smell had let him down for the first time.

Devin tackled his brother with a forceful blow to his shoulder and injured arm, crashing to the floor on top of him. He aimed for his throat, so he could tear it out.

Gabriel let out a yelp of pain and delivered a blow of his own to Devin's jaw before he could bite into him.

He was just as strong as Devin, and it was proving to be an even battle. He growled at him, "I'm going to have her, too, my brother. I've already tasted her sweet blood."

Devin, consumed with fury, used the flat of his hand to deliver a violent punch, pushing Gabriel's chin upward to expose his throat, and he went for it. "You will not touch her!" he bellowed just as his teeth broke the skin on Gabriel's throat.

As soon as his brother bit into his exposed skin, Gabriel used all of his strength and bucked his hips. Then he used both fists to punch Devin in his chest, sending him flying across the room. Once freed, he hopped up with blood spilling from his neck and chuckled, "She's mine now." He dashed away before Devin could catch him.

Gabriel had, fortunately, been prepared for this battle and his otherwise mortal wound. He'd seen a dark priest—Clive from the vampire tour—and obtained the herbs and spell he'd need. He'd also gotten the blood he would need. Clive, whom he pegged as a follower the evening of the tour, gave his own wife's blood for the cause. He gave enough for the spell that is. Now, in his native tongue, Gabriel rubbed the herbs into his throat, drank the vial of blood, and chanted:

"în întunericul acestei nopți, stau în fața ochilor tăi nesfințiți. Vindecă-mă, pledez. E sângele tău malefic de care am nevoie. Un copil al noptii, a stabilit acest lucru gresit la dreapta. Toarnă-ți sângele în mine, spiritul meu ți-a fost dat. Invoc spiritele iadului pentru a face acest vampir bine. "

In the darkness of this night, I stand before your unsanctified eyes. Heal me, I plead. It's your evil blood I need. A child of the night, set this wrong thing to right. Pour your blood into me, my spirit given to thee. I invoke the spirits of hell to make this vampire well.

He immediately started feeling better. The dark magic was working just as Clive had promised it would. Sadly, this was the only batch Gabriel had, so he couldn't sustain another fatal wound, and he couldn't go back to Clive for more because he was dead. Gabriel didn't want him around to help Devin as well, and for good measure, he'd finished the wife off too.

Now it was time to find the lovers...

62

$Salena$ could hardly keep her car on the road. She was terrified to hear what Heloise must have seen. The five miles to the Gypsy's cottage seemed more like twenty, and despite her current state of panic, her eyes were feeling heavy. Finally, the small house came into view. Salena had no idea, though, that she'd been followed by a couple of wolves when she pulled into the small driveway and immediately stepped out of the car.

Heloise was standing outside on the tiny porch holding her evil eye in one hand and a voodoo doll in the other. She yelled out to Salena, "Hurry, Salena, you are in great danger! Get inside!"

Salena shut the car door and began to run, but then something utterly horrifying stopped her. She witnessed Heloise being tackled by a large brown wolf. "No!" she screamed just as the wolf bit into her friend's throat, causing blood to spurt everywhere. Then the wolf turned on her with a malicious growl.

Salena tried desperately to get back inside her car, but she didn't make it in time. She had the wind knocked out of her, and liquid fire blazed through her shoulder as teeth bit into her flesh and bone. She knew it was over when she felt hot breath and drool on her throat, but instead of being ripped into once more, her body was wracked with convulsions. Then she felt it soaring through the air before crashing into something hard. Then she felt nothing—all was black.

Devin, still shifted into a black wolf and filled with all the rage, ferocity, and fires of hell, had flown through the air and tackled Gabriel just as he was about to rip into Salena's throat. Devin's fangs gripped Gabriel's neck, and he bit down hard.

Unfortunately, Gabriel had jerked his body away in time to avoid fatal contact. He yelped loud enough to wake the dead, though, so damage had definitely been inflicted once again. However, he escaped before Devin could deliver the final blow. Of course, that meant he didn't get to finish off Salena.

Devin rushed to his love's side, and he carried her into the Gypsy's house, pressing his shirt on her shoulder to slow down the bleeding. It took all of his restraint because her blood was calling to him like the singing of a thousand angels. His love, blessedly, overcame his thirst, though.

He laid her down on the sofa and knelt before her, weeping hard, which he had not done since Abigail was taken from him. He had not been able to save Abigail, but he would not let Salena die. He wracked his brain, trying to think of something he could chant, something he could do—something from the old world. He had certainly been around long enough to have learned something! The old Gypsy woman surely had tools that would help: potions, herbs, spells, anything to save his soulmate. He ran through her cottage grabbing books and rummaging through her cupboards for anything useful. He came across bottles of thyme, burdock root, ginger, and belladonna root, which reminded him of something he had learned during the black plague. He grabbed the bottles and ran back to Salena's side. He rubbed the ingredients into her wound while chanting an old Romanian healing spell:

"Cer soarta cu puterea de a transforma timpul înapoi pentru a salva ceea ce a fost pierdut şi, din nou, să-l a mea.

Prin timp şi spaţiu, lasă-ţi magia să-mi aducă înapoi soarta, sănătatea ei restaurată."

I beg the Fates with the power to turn back time to save what has been lost and, again, make it mine. Through time and space, let your magic soar. Bring back my fate, her health restored.

Then he waited...

63

Salena's eyes fluttered open. She was waking up in the worst pain of her entire life, and her head was foggy. Trying to focus her eyes on her surroundings, she first became aware that she was in Heloise's parlor. Secondly, she heard someone else breathing. She slowly turned her head, fighting the agonizing pain in her left shoulder. She expected to see Heloise, but she looked into a pair of black eyes instead, and she jumped, sending more searing pain through her body while a flashback of poor Heloise went through her mind.

"You!" she screamed at him. "You killed her!" She struggled to get up, but the pain was unbearable.

"No," he said softly, "it was Gabriel, not me. I'm sorry I didn't stop him in time. I'll never forgive myself for allowing him to hurt you or your friend."

Again, Salena struggled to get away, but the pain and the vampire both held her down. "Are you going to kill me too? Just get it over with!"

The terror in her eyes made tears slowly stream from his. He had to make her see and understand their connection, and he had to do it right then. With a featherlight touch, he stroked her face, which caused her to flinch and pull away, but he continued. He traced his fingers down her neck and to her injured shoulder, which was no longer bleeding.

"I'm not going to hurt you. I love you. I want to protect you from evil like the man who was attacking you in his car the other night and from my brother, Gabriel, who wants to take you away from me."

Salena blinked rapidly, as if that would change the sight before her. Then she focused—really focused—on his face. "That wasn't a dream." It came out halfway as an accusation and halfway as a question. "You were there."

She looked down at her clothing, wincing at the massive blood stain, and then at her breast. She couldn't see the bite mark because it was on the underside, but she knew it was still there. She also knew it was faded by now. She twitched and looked at him with eyes full of terror and suspicion.

"You are the vampire?" She said it like she didn't already know the answer, like she hadn't known the answer for some time now. But she wanted to hear him admit it.

He looked at her with a soft expression. "Yes, I am a vampire, and you weren't dreaming when we made love."

She squirmed away from him, pressing against the back of the sofa, and whimpered.

He brushed his hand through her hair. "I'm more than a vampire, though. I'm your destiny, and you are mine. You know this to be true—you saw it in the cards."

Salena gasped in surprise, how would he know that? Has he been following her? Every time she visited a fortuneteller or Heloise, was he watching? Then she remembered what he did to Madame Marietta, and she got angrier.

"You killed Madame Marietta too!" she screamed, and it vibrated off the cottage walls.

Her words tore through his heart because they were true, and he'd not wanted to take the Gypsy's life. "I will explain about her, but not now. We must leave because Gabriel will be back. I healed your shoulder, and it will quickly get better, but it will continue to hurt some in the meantime."

"What?" she yelped.

She looked down at her pained shoulder and remembered being bitten by a wolf—the same wolf that had killed Heloise. She saw where the bite had been, but it appeared to be rapidly healing. It wasn't even bleeding anymore. Her pain, she realized, was becoming tolerable too.

She looked up at him and whispered, "How?"

"Another question for later," he said, scooping her up. "We must go now. Gabriel will heal quickly as well, and he will come back for us soon."

Before she could object or ask any more questions, they were out the door and running through the woods. Salena winced over Heloise's body and turned her head into his musky shoulder. *His?* She didn't even know his name.

"Who are you? And why do you say we are destined? What the hell is this all about? And we can't leave her there! And what about my car? Put me down! I want to go home!" Her words ran together and almost sounded garbled.

Devin ignored both her questions and her demand. Tossing her over his shoulder, he ran so fast it made her head spin.

Salena pummeled her fists against his back. He had no right to just run off with her and leave her poor friend dead in front of her house. And he didn't bother to answer her questions.

Devin stopped and put her down, but he held her in place by her shoulders, being tender with her left side. She squirmed to get away, and he growled at her. "Stop! Just listen to me." He didn't want to be gruff with her, but she needed to listen before it was too late for the both of them. Softly, he continued, "You have to understand you are in danger. We are both in great danger from Gabriel. He will be coming back, and I have to be ready for him. Sit down, and I will attempt to explain some of this to you."

She sat down because she was far too scared to try to run away. She watched him curiously as he reached into his pocket and produced her cell phone.

"You can call the police about your friend. You can even tell them about me if you like; although, they won't catch us," he told her and held her phone out.

She believed him and took the phone. She blocked her phone number under the phone's settings, and then she made an anonymous report to the police about poor Heloise. She told them she came across the body while hiking, and that she thought the woman had been attacked by some kind of animal.

She had no idea what the police would think about her car still being at Heloise's house, though, especially so late in the evening. She looked at the clock on her phone; it was already 1:00 in the morning. How long was she unconscious? It seemed like she was at the restaurant with Eric only a few minutes ago. And *he* had been there too...

Turning back to her captor, she continued with her demands. "Now, explain all of this to me, including why my friend is dead! And did you do something to Eric?"

Devin knew she was furious, and it was time to explain things. Taking a deep breath, he began calmly, "My name is Devin. Some of the victims were my—for the lack of a better word—dinner. Some of them were Gabriel's."

Salena interrupted, "Who is Gabriel, and why is he after me?"

"He is my brother, and he's after us because—" he stopped, trying to think of the right words. "—It all has to do with the past. It involves your great-grandmother Abigail. I know you've heard about her and my connection to her."

Salena interrupted him again. "Yeah, about that, how do you know that, and how do you know I'm her relative?"

Devin sighed deeply. "Please let me answer all of your questions without interruption. We are in a hurry here."

Feeling like a scolded child, she blushed with a nod.

"I have been keeping an eye on you because you *are mine*. You are destined as my soulmate, and I have to protect you and keep others from interfering." He saw her mouth start to open, so he held up his large hand to squelch her. "Abigail is—well, was—my truelove. Gabriel wanted to take her away from me, so he attacked her. I was there in time to save her, though, and I'm going to save you too." Tears filled his eyes, and sadness overwhelmed him. "I just wasn't in time to save her from *them*."

Salena also looked solemn. She knew to whom he was referring—the colonists. She looked at Devin and was surprised to see tears rolling down his exquisitely perfect face. She would never have expected a vampire to cry. Then again, she would never have expected a vampire to fall in love, but of course, she never suspected they existed at all. What an insane vacation it has been for her. She rubbed her temples as he continued.

"Now, regarding the fortuneteller, she sought me out. She had foreseen her looming traumatic death and thought I could help her transition peacefully. She begged me to end her life. Believe me, please, that I hated killing her, especially because she told you we belong together."

Salena wasn't sure she believed him, until she saw another tear roll down. *Who knew vampires could feel remorse? Unless he's a good faker...*Nonetheless, she let him continue.

"Now, as to why you have been told we are destined"—he gave her a deep smoldering look—"as I said, Abigail was my truelove, and she would have been my savior, but she, as you know, was burned alive. They burned her because they believed she practiced witchcraft, which she didn't. A vampire doesn't usually fall in love, so when he or she does, it is truly magical; they are given a rare opportunity, which I am not going to go into with you right now because you are not ready. Abigail's blood runs through you, and the physical similarities are impeccable. It is like you are her, reincarnated—I would swear she was standing before me."

Salena didn't know what to think. It wasn't the first time somebody had mentioned reincarnation to her, so what should she believe?

"So, I look like her," she stated flatly, "and maybe I taste like her, which is gross, and I don't appreciate you biting me, by the way, but how does that make me your soulmate? And, just for the record, I don't believe in reincarnation." On a side note to herself, she added, *but I do, apparently, believe in vampires and fortunetellers.*

Devin didn't have time to answer her question, though, because he could smell Gabriel closing in on them. He used to be able to pick up another vampire's scent from several hundred yards away. However, since he hadn't been around any others for such a long time, he didn't trust his instincts anymore. He grabbed Salena's arm and picked her up, cradling her over his arms this time, and began to run again. He explained to her that Gabriel was getting closer, and they had to go.

That didn't settle her nerves, and the bouncing certainly didn't settle her stomach.

Gabriel smelled his brother and the mortal woman; they weren't more than five hundred yards away. Devin must have found some way to heal her shoulder because she should have already bled out. Her blood, he remembered, was so sweet. He wanted more of it, and he definitely wanted to have her luscious body. Maybe he'd make Devin watch while he repeatedly ravaged her before draining her completely. He may not have been able to finish what he had started with Abigail, but this time, he would, and Devin would be crushed all over again. Running through the trees, shifted into a brown wolf, he sought them out.

After about twenty minutes of vigorous running, Gabriel decided to have a snack. He headed toward the highway, shifted back into human form, and pretended to be hitchhiking. The first car to stop had two young females in it. Either their parents hadn't warned them about picking up hitchhikers or they just didn't care to listen. They grinned up at him like fools, and he could tell they'd been drinking. He could smell the alcohol on them.

"Where are you headed?" the driver slurred a little as he climbed into the back seat.

He replied with a wicked grin, "Oh, it's not far."

He grabbed her by her hair and pulled her to his fangs. The girl in the passenger seat jumped out, screaming and running as fast as she could, but it wasn't fast enough. In no time at all, he'd caught up to her and drained her too. It took both of the slim girls to fill him up.

Back to the hunt...

65

Devin changed directions and headed northwest, but eventually, he would turn back toward New Orleans. It was late morning, and they were hidden in the woods near a subdivision. He scanned the backyards for food for Salena—he had heard her stomach growling over the pounding of his footsteps and her constant complaining. He noticed an apple tree in one yard and a barbeque pit cooking meat in another.

Setting her down, he told her sternly, "Now, I'm going to get you some food, so stay put. You know I will catch you if you run off, right?"

She nodded slowly without making eye contact. She knew what would happen if she tried to run, and she was hungry. She was hungry and exhausted.

"Okay. I'll be right back." He gave her another look of warning before he walked off.

She wondered what to think about him. *Why does he think he's in love with me? What am I supposed to do now?* Her head was spinning and not just from low blood sugar.

He returned with a grilled pork steak and an apple for her, which she ravenously ate. She didn't even mind burning her mouth on the hot meat.

"Thank you," she told him softly.

"You're very welcome. You have a little barbecue sauce on your lip." He reached out and tenderly wiped it away with his fingertip.

Her tongue traced where his finger had been. It was only a reflex, but it excited him, and she heard his quick intake of breath. She shyly looked away. She was feeling better with food in her stomach, but her head was pounding, so she rubbed her temples and scalp.

"Do you have a headache?" he asked with concern.

She looked up at him, squinting. "Yes."

"Here, let me help."

He gently brushed her hands away, replacing them with his, and they were warm and strong. He rubbed her temples and all around her scalp and neck. She moaned with pleasure from his touch, and he knew his hands were working magic on her. He leaned down in front of her, so he could give her a deep kiss. To his surprise, she returned his kiss with just as much passion and without any hypnotic spells. Their mouths remained locked, exploring each other intimately until she had to come up for air.

Salena blushed and bashfully turned her head away. She knew she shouldn't have gotten carried away like that. The kiss had turned her on, though, and she knew it had turned him on, too, because as soon as he stood up, she saw a bulge in his pants, and it made her blush deepen.

He noticed her red cheeks and chuckled, "No need for modesty about that. That's what happens when I'm near you, and that kiss was wonderful, wasn't it?"

Salena nodded because she knew he saw the shame on her face. The kiss had been amazing, and it made her flash back to her dream, which he'd admitted wasn't a dream after all. Trying to redeem her modesty, though, she couldn't help but explain herself.

"That was just my reaction to the massage. It felt really nice, and my head is better, so thank you."

"Oh, okay," he responded with an amused grin. "We should travel now." He helped her up off the ground and gave her hand a gentle squeeze.

Salena was glad to change the topic, but she didn't want to travel anymore. "But I'm tired. Can't we rest for a bit?" She looked up at him with pleading eyes.

"I'll cradle you in my arms, so you can rest. I promise to walk gently, so it will be like rocking you to sleep."

Salena looked around nervously. "I need to use the ladies' room. I don't suppose you have one of those in your bag of tricks, do you? Speaking of which, I want to know how you healed my shoulder."

He looked at her with a wide grin. "Well, haven't you ever been camping? There are bushes over there you can use, and I'll give you some privacy."

She looked to where he pointed and scowled. "There are snakes over there, and camping is not how I wanted to spend my vacation." *And neither is being chased by vampires.*

Devin strolled to the bushes and looked around. "No snakes or critters," he hollered back to her. "You are good to go, pun intended." He laughed heartily, and so did she.

His sense of humor dumbfounded her. Maybe vampires weren't all doom and gloom. But then she thought about his brother, Gabriel, and the woman he had killed right before the crowd's very eyes without any fear of being caught. She also thought about him attacking her in the fog and then, of course, Heloise. He definitely was all doom and gloom. But aside from Devin's extraordinary features, and the fact that he had drunk her blood a few times, he almost seemed human. He resembled a man trying to win her love.

After doing her business, Salena put her arms around Devin's neck, so he could pick her up and carry her. She was exhausted, and his arms and shoulders were very inviting and surprisingly soft enough given his size and strength. He cradled her gently and walked with even strides with minimal bounce. As she started to drift off to sleep, lulled by his enticing musky fragrance, she noticed his heartbeat. She looked up at him through half-closed eyes.

"How can you have a heartbeat?" Her eyebrows were pulled together.

He murmured hypnotically, "It beats for you."

"That's sweet," she whispered before falling asleep.

Devin traveled back toward New Orleans with Salena safely nestled in his arms. His heart fluttered from her closeness to it. It was time—time to explain the secrets of their bond, of their destiny. He had to do it soon before Gabriel could stop it.

He stopped at an old abandoned farmhouse. The night had a chill in the air, and despite his body heat, he could feel her shiver. Being careful not to wake her, he laid her down in the grass. Fortunately, she was so exhausted that she didn't really seem to notice. The cold ground made her shiver more, though, and in her sleep she was reaching for something—like her blanket perhaps. Devin took off his shirt and cocooned her in it. Then he grabbed some kindling and rocks and built an old-fashioned fire for her. Sitting there, watching her smile in her sleep from the warmth of the fire, his heart quivered. The glow from the fire framed her delicate porcelain-like features and reminded him once more of Abigail; however, the pain was less—a lot less. The transition was taking place. His love for Abigail was being displaced by his love for Salena.

Her eyes flickered open, and she abruptly sat up. Devin, her captor and vampire, was sitting across from her, staring and shirtless. His broad muscular chest glistened in the firelight, and she felt a pleasant tingle run down her spine and settle between her legs. She looked down and found his shirt wrapped around her.

"Where are we, and why am I wrapped in your shirt?" Her voice trembled because she couldn't help but enjoy both the view of his bare chest and his heady scent on the shirt encasing her.

"We are at an old farm, and you're wearing my shirt because you were cold. I think it looks good on you too." He gave her a sexy grin and a wink.

Meekly looking down, she told him, "Thank you, but aren't you cold?"

"No, temperature doesn't bother me."

Salena looked around the darkness, trying to get a feel for her surroundings. She pulled her cell phone out of her pocket, but there was no signal. She had no idea where they were or even what day it was. She felt like she had been asleep for days.

"Your stomach is growling," he pointed out. "Let me catch something for you to eat, and then I can cook it for you on the fire. You'll eat squirrel or rabbit, won't you?" he asked with another wink.

Normally she wouldn't; however, considering her surroundings, her circumstances, and the fact that she was with a vampire, who might also be hungry, she acquiesced, "Sure. That's fine."

Devin hopped up and walked off toward the woods. At the edge, he abruptly stopped and turned around to look at her. "Don't you even think about running off. I'll catch you and put you over my knee."

Salena couldn't tell if he was being serious or not, but she nodded. "I won't," she promised.

She couldn't stop from admiring the smooth muscled planes of his back and his sexy buttocks as he walked away in long graceful strides. He must have felt her staring because he looked over his shoulder and flashed her a wicked smile. With her cheeks blazing, she immediately dropped her shameful gaze to the ground.

Devin returned about five minutes later and held up a squirrel for her approval.

"That was fast," she said with a grimace.

"Don't worry; it tastes like chicken," he laughed.

She giggled and shook her head. "That is never true when people say that."

"No, it's not, is it? But it will have to do for now." He shoved a stick through the carcass and put it on the fire.

"That's gross." She nervously looked up at him and quietly asked, "What are you going to eat?"

He gave her a grin that showed off his fangs while his eyes looked up and down her body. "I'm thinking about eating *you* right now."

Salena scrambled backward like a caged animal, but she knew she would never get away. In fact, he had already jumped over the fire to stand right in front of her.

"I'm getting hard from just thinking about it. Look." He cupped himself and chuckled. He knew she'd misunderstood him.

The innuendo finally dawned on Salena, and her cheeks flamed hotter than the fire. "So, you don't mean to drain me of my blood? Or are you just waiting? If so, please just get it over with." She extended her arm toward him, and he erupted in laughter.

"Why would I kill you? While the flavor of your blood is like nothing I've tasted before—well, not since Abigail—I wouldn't dare drain you of it. You are my soulmate. You came back to me, so we can finish our destiny." He took her arm and started kissing his way up it.

She pulled away in protest. "Don't do that."

Devin grinned his fangs at her again. "You didn't mind before. Actually, you rather enjoyed yourself"—he sucked air in quickly and closed his eyes—"I remember the look on your face and the way you smelled." He breathed in deeply and growled, "I loved the way you sounded and the way you felt—mmm...so good." He focused his lust-filled black eyes on her and gently placed her hand on his rock-hardness. "See for yourself," he moaned.

Admittedly, touching him intimately put butterflies in her tummy and a tingle at the apex of her legs, but she still pulled her hand away out of shyness. Then memories flooded back to her, and she became angry.

"You tricked me. I don't know how, but you did something to me. That wasn't really me!" she yelled at him.

Refusing to give up, Devin inched closer to her. "Oh, it was you. It was you letting go of your stubbornness. It was the part of you that knows we are meant to be. It was the part of you that knows I am your destiny, and you are mine. It was definitely you." He leaned down and whispered softly in her ear, "And it can be again"—he kissed her earlobe—"It will be"—he kissed her neck—"It's meant to be." He turned her face and kissed her full on the lips.

She wanted to stop him, but she found herself kissing him back. She didn't know if it was her fear, the setting by the fire, his half-nakedness, or her memories of their previous encounters, but she let herself get swept up in his kiss. She put her hands around his neck while his began to roam under his shirt, which was still wrapped around her. The intimate touch made her nervous, though, so she broke away.

"I can't," she stated flatly. "I still don't understand this." She pointed to the fire. "My dinner is done."

Swept up in lust, Devin had forgotten about the squirrel, which appeared to be a lot more than done—it was burnt to a crisp. He removed it from the fire, and with his bare hands, he peeled back the outer layer of skin to get to the meat inside. He blew on the hot meat to cool it for his love and then offered it to her. He still held it, though, just in case it was still too hot for her.

She didn't know what to think. He was just full of surprises. She took the meat with a polite, "Thank you," and ate it in just a few bites. It definitely wasn't to her liking, but she was hungry enough not to complain about it.

He sat down next to her and tried to think of the right words to finish his explanation. He looked at her fixedly. "You doubt we are meant to be together, despite having your future explained to you by multiple sources, despite the things you have seen, and despite what I've told you. But I understand; it is a different reality than what you are used to. So, I have been patient and have slowly tried to bring you around to the idea. That's why I used some spells on you." He saw her expression turn from inquisitive to angry. "A spell also healed your shoulder. It was a fatal wound."

His words made her wince, and she looked at her shoulder. It was just a faint scar now and didn't hurt any longer.

"And I could tell you enjoyed my love making," he added with his vampire grin. "And while I couldn't avoid taking your gorgeous body in pleasure, it was *making love*."

Salena blushed again and looked away from his mysterious black eyes. The truth was, she had enjoyed it— a lot.

"The love I shared with Abigail was something the world had never seen before and would probably never see again. People can write all the love stories they want, but it was not just a storybook fantasy. It was transcendent. We were bound to one another—destined soulmates—swept up in a magical force that was stronger than both of us, and it was only interrupted by her death. But"—he pointed to her—"not destroyed. When I bit your wrist in the phone booth, I tasted her blood in you. It startled me, and that's why I ran away. There was a familiarity, but I wasn't sure what it was at the time. Then the second encounter—" He saw the questioning look on her face and paused. "—No, that wasn't a dream either, but you probably already knew that. During that encounter, I saw the physical likeness as well, and that is when I knew you had to be her—or her descendant anyway. Her bloodline still holds that magic; *you* still hold that magic. It is alive in you for us to intertwine once more."

Salena could only stare at him. She was mesmerized by both his story and his striking features. His face was glowing in the morning sun, which was peaking over the horizon.

She had millions of questions but decided to start with, "Why is Gabriel after me?"

Devin stood up and reached his hand out to help her up before answering her. "Because he wants what I love. He always has. Now, I know you have more questions, and I have more answers, but now we must leave. We must head back toward New Orleans and go to the Gulf of Mexico. I'm going to put out the fire. You can relieve yourself over by that barn." He pointed toward the structure.

She did need to go, so she headed off toward the barn. When she got back, she looked up at him—he was a good nine or ten inches taller than her. "Are we going back to my house then?"

He looked remorseful and ashamed. "No, Gabriel destroyed your house, and he would look for us there anyway." After seeing the hurt expression on her face, he quickly added, "I will fix your house for you and replace its contents, so please don't worry."

All she could feel was worry. She was full of worry and terror.

"I will carry you again because it's much faster that way. You can sleep some more if you like."

She reached up around his neck, and he cradled her in his arms again. "Tell me about Abigail, please."

Devin smiled the biggest smile she'd seen on him yet. "Abigail was the most beautiful woman I'd ever seen, even to this day. Well, until you—you are the mirror image of her, and I should've recognized it that night in the phone booth. I guess my heart had blocked it out after three hundred years of pain and agony. She was beautiful, kind, mischievous, sexy, and a terrific mom to her son, Graham."

Salena remembered seeing the name Graham Saunders on her family tree.

Devin went on, "She was funny and full of love and life. It was so wrong of them to condemn her. I wanted to destroy all of them, too, but Graham needed a place to grow up, and his uncle begged me to walk away. He wanted to move to another village and raise the child without their name being tarnished and following them. So, I walked away out of my concern for the boy." He looked down at her, and she was sleeping like an angel—his angel.

Salena was in the forest again, but this time, it was light outside, and no terrible creatures were following her. Best of all, there was no dark shadow. She looked around and saw a woman walking in a clearing. As she got closer to the woman, she realized she was staring at Abigail. She knew it was her because they looked alike, but the woman was wearing clothing from a different century.

Salena tried to run toward her tenth-generation great-grandmother, but she felt held in place. She was desperate to ask her about Devin and her romance with him. She had so many questions for her dead relative.

Abigail finally turned in her direction, and she waved for her to come closer. Salena felt like her feet were stuck in the mud, though, and she couldn't move. Then suddenly, she felt arms around her; it was Devin, and he carried her to the clearing and set her down.

Abigail was looking in a different direction, though, and when Salena approached her and saw what she was staring at, the scene shocked her. Angry people with lit torches were running toward Abigail.

"Witch!" they shouted. Then they turned on Salena and pointed. "She's a witch too! Burn her alive. Burn them both!"

Salena reached for Abigail's hand, so they could run away, but when she grabbed it, Abigail turned to her, exposing vicious vampire fangs, and lunged. Devin, meanwhile, stood there and watched.

With a jerk, Salena woke up and almost fell out of Devin's arms. He was able to catch her, though, and maintain his hold before she hit the ground. She struggled to get away, so he gently set her down.

"What's wrong?" He was genuinely concerned.

"I will not become one of you! I don't care if Abigail wanted to; I don't!" She backed away from him while shouting and then broke into a run.

He immediately caught up to her and threw her over his shoulder, and she pummeled her fists against his back again. He tolerated her assault and kept her tightly in place.

"I don't know what you're talking about, Salena, but I'm guessing you had a nightmare. I won't put you down until you calm down and tell me what you're upset about," he told her sternly.

"I'm not going to let you turn me into a vampire!" she shrieked and continued to pound her fists, even though they hurt from hitting his hard muscle.

He stopped walking and put her down, but he maintained a firm grasp. "Listen"—he stared into her angry but captivating blue eyes—"I'm not turning anyone into a vampire. I've never turned anyone into a vampire."

Salena was confused. "How could you live with Abigail then? How could you be together? That doesn't make any sense."

Devin took a deep breath, "Do you remember when I told you that Abigail was my savior, but now you are my savior?"

She shrugged her slender shoulders. "Maybe. I think so."

"Okay, I'll explain. Abigail was my savior because our bonds of love contained a magical power hidden within the supernatural realm. It had nothing to do with turning her into a vampire. The strength of our love had the ability to return something to me that I had lost long before we'd met—my mortality. She, through her love, had the ability to make me human again. We were going to be together as humans—both of us."

"What?" she yelped. She was utterly confused. "How is that possible?"

"The purity of truelove is something that is hard to achieve. Yes, people fall in love, but it's rare to find your soulmate," he explained. "Only with a soulmate, can a human find his or her true enlightenment and transcend beyond the realm of normal human love. But with a vampire, that magic is at least one hundred-fold. To turn a vampire mortal again is unlike any magic experienced in either of our worlds. Her love—your love—has the power to return my soul to me."

"Wow, that is intense. But, unfortunately, I'm not in love. I don't see how I could let myself fall in love with a vampire. You kill people, Devin. In fact, you killed Jane, didn't you?"

Devin looked away from her accusing gaze. "Yes, I killed your friend Jane because she wanted to interfere by introducing you to Rob, who turned out to be a rapist, so I rescued you from him. I understand you are upset about your friend, and I apologize. That's why I left the flowers, but that turned out to be a big mistake, so I apologize for that as well. Our love is more important than that friendship, though, and time was of the essence. You already had your own superstitions and beliefs that I needed to overcome, and apparently, I still do.

"Now, you say you are not in love, but Abigail's love—the love we had shared together—is alive in you. I felt it when we made love, and the Gypsies and priestess saw it. You just have walls put up to block your view of it. Standing in front of you is a man—a man deeply in love. I knew about your readings because I watched you, protected you, learned about you, and fell in love with you. You carry Abigail inside you. You are Abigail whether you choose to believe that or not."

Salena chose her words carefully before stating her argument. "No, I am not Abigail; I am Salena. You can't love me because of whom you think I am or whom I remind you of. I am not her, and I can't become her. This is three hundred years later—a different time, a different place, and a different woman."

"A different woman, yes, but it's the same love. It never died, Salena; it was reborn in you. I recently just came back to New Orleans. This is the first time I've been here since Abigail's death. I didn't know why I needed to come back until after I got here. I didn't know why until I bit you. You brought me here, to my place of pain, so I could be reborn—so I can have a soul and live a life filled with love with you."

Salena shook her head and rubbed her temples. She felt another migraine coming on. *How can I respond to this without breaking his heart? Love can't be forced, yet he's telling me it's there whether I want it or not.* She was tired of everyone telling her how her life was going to be as if she had no say on the subject. It didn't seem to matter what she decided— she had to go with what history had decided for her.

Devin understood her turmoil, and he felt bad about it. He wished the situation was easier for her. He wished he had better explanations and better answers for her.

"You must be tired now, and we're almost to New Orleans, so would you like to rest?" he questioned.

"Yes," she agreed. "A nap sounds great. It's just what I need." They were standing in a grassy plain with nothing else in sight but a small wooded area, so she lay down on the grass and closed her eyes.

"Okay, you rest while I hunt in those woods," he told her.

"You're going to hunt people, aren't you?"

"Well, yes, I'm still a vampire for the moment."

Disgusted, she let it go at that and closed her eyes again. The situation wasn't desirable, but at least he wasn't hunting her. She heard him walk away just as she felt the pull of slumber.

Gabriel couldn't believe his luck; he had tracked the lovers down, and now his brother had left Salena alone. It would take Devin a long time to hunt down prey in the scarce woods. He should know because he had already been through them. *No matter. I'll eat well now.*

He approached the sleeping lass. She was curled up sweetly on the ground and softly snoring. He lay down behind her and started caressing her shoulder, which made her smile in her sleep. She was likely thinking her lover had returned to her.

Gabriel murmured, "Sunteti sub controlul meu," *You are under my control.* He wanted her aware of the situation but helpless to do anything about it. Then he started to rip her clothes.

Salena's eyes flew open; she couldn't tell if she was dreaming or not, but either way, she didn't like it. At first, she thought Devin had returned to her and was trying to get her to make love. But then she was forcefully rolled onto her back to come face-to-face with someone else. He grinned, and she immediately recognized him from the vampire tour. He was Devin's brother, Gabriel. She opened her mouth to scream but couldn't—it was like she had been drugged. She knew she was under a spell.

"Shh…" he told her. "You don't want to do that. Just enjoy."

Gabriel ran his fingertips over her body, which was still too heavily clothed, so he ripped them some more to expose her. Then he started planting hot nips on her skin. Kissing was for lovers, and he was not going to be her lover.

Salena wanted to pull away, wanted to run away, and wanted to scream, but she couldn't do anything. She felt like his puppet—helpless and his to do with as he wished.

"Turn over," Gabriel growled aggressively.

His flesh was rigid for her now. He would use her more than he had ever used a woman before, and when he killed her, he would do it slowly. Abigail had denied him, and this woman—her descendent—would suffer for it.

Without any control over her own actions, Salena followed the vampire's instructions and turned herself over for him. He had already ripped her shorts off, and she felt his molten member prod the opening to her dry womanhood. He wasn't gentle about it either. His thrusts tore into her, and she felt like her passage was on fire. Then a new pain blinded her—his fangs. He'd sank his fangs into the back of her shoulder while he rode her hard. Again, she tried to scream, and again, there was nothing.

Gabriel drove into her with the force of ten men and filled her to the hilt. He rammed her with all his strength knowing, of course, that he was hurting her. Good. He succumbed to his thirst and bit down hard into her shoulder. His mouth filled with her warm, sweet blood, and as her life essence flowed down into his stomach, he already felt stronger and more virile. Then his fiery culmination was upon him, and he flooded her. Devin's whore absorbed every drop of his seed.

Deciding it wasn't enough gratification, though, he flipped her over and continued his onslaught. He pressed her right knee up toward her chest, and then he once again impaled her on his straining shaft. Smiling, he leaned down and kissed her hard on the mouth with his bloody lips.

Salena tried to struggle, to scream, to get away, but she was defenseless. He'd paralyzed her but, unfortunately, not from the pain. Her body was on fire.

Gabriel moved from her unwelcoming mouth to her neck and bit deep, spilling her blood down his throat once again. The delectable liquid made his body glow with excitement and vitality. For the first time, he could understand Devin's obsession with Abigail. Nevertheless, he wouldn't have given up immortality for her.

He decided it wasn't the right time to kill Salena. It was going to be more fun for him when Devin found her like this: used, bitten, and almost drained. It was going to be torturous for Devin to see that he couldn't protect any of his women. His heart would break when he learned he was a failure. So, after one last small satisfying drink from her, Gabriel left her lying there in her miserable state of disrepair.

Devin was on his way back to Salena from his hunting trip. Luckily, he had found a couple of hunters, and one was a woman. She wasn't much, and the man was worse, but they would have to hold him over until he got back to New Orleans. As he came upon the field where he'd left Salena, he could sense something was wrong—he could sense Gabriel. He darted across the grassy field to her side. She was lying there half-naked, bleeding, and motionless. His heart felt like it was ripped from his chest. If he was too late...

He checked her wrist and felt a faint pulse, so he thanked God for that. He took off his shirt and covered her nakedness. Blood was still escaping from Gabriel's bite marks, so he ripped off pieces of her tattered clothing to press down on the wounds. Again, he had to fight hard to deny his own inner demons that wanted to drink. Then for the second time in the past forty-eight hours, he thought hard about a spell. There had to be something, anything. Picking her up, he carried her gently into the woods.

Devin searched the woods for various herbs, roots, and anything that might be useful. He came across an old willow tree, and that gave him an idea. Laying her gently on the ground, he took some branches from the willow tree, broke them off into twigs, and used the leaves to bind them together—he made a voodoo doll. Hoping it would work, he put the voodoo doll up against her throat and chanted a spell:

> *Vampiri psihic in noapte*
> *Vampiri psihic care distruge viata mea*
> *Distruge nu mai mult de ceea ce am realiza*
> *Distruge nu mai mult de ceea ce primesc*
> *Negativitatea nu este binevenit*
> *Răul nu este binevenit*
> *În mine, în apropiere de mine sau de oameni*
> *pe care îmi locul.*

It was a voodoo spell to ward off vampires and their magic. While chanting it, he could tell it was helping her, but he was burning from the inside out because it warded off all vampires. It was hurting him, maybe even killing him, but it would be worth it to save her.

Salena felt a burning sensation in her shoulder, neck, and between her legs, but it was getting lighter and less noticeable. She had no idea where she was, or whom she was with when she slowly opened her eyes. Once she focused them, she could see Devin lying next to her and writhing in pain. She saw the voodoo doll drop to the ground when she sat up. Then she noticed she was wearing his blood-stained shirt over her tattered clothing, and she remembered, with perfect clarity, Gabriel's attack. Shudders wracked her body, but it no longer hurt. Her pain had magically disappeared.

But why is Devin in pain? Did he fight his brother? Did he absorb my pain?

She rushed to his side and looked into his midnight eyes, and for reasons she didn't understand, she kissed him.

Devin felt like his insides were on fire; he felt like he would explode at any second. Then with just her kiss, it was miraculously gone. It was replaced by a glowing warmth. He openly responded to her kiss, pulling her in deep before rolling her onto her back, and lying down on top of her.

Forgetting the trauma she'd just endured, Salena surrendered to the flow of passion and welcomed his embrace, his kiss, and more that she was sure would come. She clawed at his bare chest and marveled at his powerful muscular frame. He was so incredibly male. She planted heated kisses on his chest while her hands roamed lower on his body—over his taut abs, over his strong hips, to between his muscular thighs—where she cupped his hard male heat. She was once again amazed at the wondrous size of him, and once again, she couldn't wait to have his pulsing sex inside her. This time, though, it was of her own free will. It felt like something was driving her, but it was not like the haze before.

Her shorts, or what was left of them, were already off, and she tugged at the opening of his pants while he kissed her deeply and passionately. Freeing his hot distended flesh, she slowly and deliciously guided him inside her body. There was no more pain there. There was only her urgent desire to welcome him into her needful core.

Devin groaned in delight from the feel of her. As her center of paradise welcomed him, he played with her delectable rosy tips, pinching them gently, and cupping her creamy soft mounds. He took one bud into his mouth, suckling and causing screams of enjoyment from her. Then once she was wet enough, he plunged himself the rest of the way inside her passion-soaked depths.

Salena saw starbursts behind her closed eyelids, and then she opened her eyes to focus them on his. His black eyes were more like a murky purple, filled with passion and desire. His fangs were glistening in the sunset, and for some reason, she wanted to feel them. "Bite me, Devin. Please, I want you to."

Incredibly surprised by her request, especially after what she'd just went through with Gabriel, Devin hesitated.

"Please," she begged.

He very gently bit into her breast, avoiding all major veins, and let tiny droplets of blood spill into his mouth—all without going too deep, without drinking too much. Her flavor quickened his pulse and made him come alive with a strength he never knew he had. He felt the beast inside him tearing to get out. He felt their bond strengthening and forming—completely—he felt loved.

Salena woke up in Devin's arms. Her head was resting on his chest, and his arm was tightly wrapped around her. For the first time since she'd met him, she felt content and not afraid. Something felt right about being with him. She had no idea why, but she didn't want to fight the feeling.

Devin felt Salena stir and looked at her, wondering what she was thinking. She wasn't trying to pull away, so it was a positive sign. Testing the waters, he gave her a squeeze, and she responded by nuzzling closer. He didn't want to disturb the moment, but he knew they had to leave.

"We must go now. We have to get to the ocean before it's too late," he informed her.

"You have said that before about the ocean. Why is that?"

Devin mentally chastised himself for letting Gabriel get to her while he was hunting. It was his job to protect her, and he had failed—like he had failed with

Abigail. No, not like with Abigail; Salena was alive and well, and she was going to stay that way.

"I have to lead Gabriel to the ocean. There are only two sure ways to kill a vampire—ripping out their throat or submersing them in salt water. He is extremely resourceful and strong, and he survived my last attack on him, so I plan to do both to him next time to finish this once and for all. I have to do it while I'm still a vampire, or I won't be able to stop him."

Salena looked at him thoughtfully. "Will you get to keep the purple eyes?"

Devin's eyebrows rose in surprise and fear. His eyes had only appeared purple once before in his entire existence—when Abigail fell in love with him. It might already be too late, in which case, the only thing they could do was run—run fast and hide.

70

Gabriel headed back to Salena's house to look for her and Devin. Sadly, they weren't there; however, the neighbors were there checking out the damage, and he just couldn't resist a quick bite. He took care of the husband first by snapping the middle-aged man's neck like a twig before tossing the body into the shrubs. The wife just stood there watching and screaming the whole time until Gabriel had killed the man, and then she finally decided it was a good time to run. She ran into their house and Gabriel could hear a lock click. Amused, he strolled after her and broke the front door down with one punch.

"Come out, come out, wherever you are," he called out in a sing-song voice. He loved playing hide-and-seek with his prey. It was much like what he was doing with Devin and his woman.

Gabriel walked through the woman's kitchen, slamming cabinet doors and drawers. He commented loudly, "My, my, my…look at all these dirty dishes. You really need to be punished for that." He strolled leisurely through her living room. "Tell me," he shouted while slamming the hall closet door just for show—he knew exactly where she was. He could smell her perfume and her fear. "Does your husband, oops…*did* your husband punish you for that?" He headed up the stairs, making sure to stomp, so she knew where he was, so she knew he was getting closer. "Did he spank you? Slap you?" Walking into the bathroom, he whisked the shower curtain aside and banged the door shut. Oh yes, she knew he was close now; he could hear her heart pounding from terror. "Did he fuck you hard? That's what I'd do. I'd take you from behind, so I could spank your pale, white ass. It is pale, isn't it?"

He tried the master bedroom door, which of course was locked. Just as he was about to break it down, he heard a cell phone ringing from downstairs. It was probably in her purse, which he'd seen hanging on the coat rack in the foyer.

"Uh, uh, uh," he chastised her while breaking down the door and spraying wood all over the plush carpet. *Such fine carpet in such a fine house nestled in a safe neighborhood...well, maybe not today.* "You left your cell phone downstairs. How, oh how, will you call the police?" He heard soft sobs coming from behind the double closet doors. "Not that they could help you, though, right? I mean, you did see what I did to your husband—how I snapped his neck with my bare hands, right?" Her sobs grew louder. "Maybe bullets won't stop me." He paced slowly to the closet while knocking items off her fancy dresser along the way. "Maybe, I'm friggin' Superman." He flicked the brass knob of the closet door with his fingernail and then pulled slowly, but the clever woman had tied the knobs together. "Maybe I'm Spiderman, or maybe"—he forced the closet door open, causing the wood to splinter—"*I'm a vampire.*"

She screamed and scrambled to get away, but he grabbed her by her hair and yanked her up to her knees.

He looked down at her with his coal-black eyes, which reminded her of a shark's. "Don't you want to play with me? Smart lady, tying the doors shut, but did you *really* think that would keep me out?" Pulling her up to her feet, he led her to the bed and shoved her down face first. He grabbed her shoulder and flipped her over. "Look at me!" he shouted. "Did you think you could keep me out?"

Sobbing, the scared witless woman shook her head side to side.

Gabriel laughed ominously and flashed his fangs. Her eyes popped out of her skull at the sight of them, and she tried to back away on the bed. He laughed again and grabbed her ankle with a reflex faster than a cobra's strike. He traced his fangs with the tip of his tongue.

"Do you like them? You look so surprised. I told you I'm a vampire. Did you think I'd lie about something that important? Take a good look because these aren't plastic, hon."

Again, the woman tried desperately to get away, but he twisted her ankle while pulling her body toward him. She yelped in pain while he pretended to soothe her.

"Don't worry. I'm not going to bite you. Well, not *yet*. I've got other plans for you first." His eyes roamed over her form. "You really aren't my type. Sorry if that hurts your feelings, dear, but"—he shrugged his shoulders—"I feel it's important to be honest with one another at times like this. Don't you?"

When she didn't respond, he twisted her ankle to the point of breaking until she nodded in agreement. "That's a good girl. Now, as I was saying, while you aren't my type, I feel sorry for you after seeing the limp dick you were married to, and you are kind of feisty. Feisty women turn me on." He unbuttoned his pants and exposed his rigid flesh as proof.

Her sobs came louder and more forceful, and she covered her eyes.

"Oh, come now. Look at me." When she didn't, he twisted her ankle again. "Look at me," he repeated sternly.

She obliged his sadistic behavior before her ankle snapped. She looked up with her tear-filled eyes and sniveled.

"Have you ever been with a man as gorgeous, as endowed, and as perfect as I am? Sure, I bet you were attractive in your younger years. What are you now about forty-five, forty-six?"

She nodded because she was afraid to anger him.

"Even back then, did you ever have a man touch you who looked like this?" He gestured his free hand over his form.

The terror-stricken woman shook her head side to side.

He chuckled vindictively. "Good girl, you told the truth. Of course, if you don't want to watch, you don't have to. Now, tell me how much you want me. Beg me," he demanded.

Her voice quaked when she replied, "No. I won't say that."

He shrugged again. "Very well, but I know that you do. So did the little bitch I ravaged earlier."

He grabbed her legs and flipped her over on her stomach. He lifted her up to her knees, yanked her pants down, and drove himself forcefully into her dry passage. The louder she screamed and cried, the harder he plunged. Before climaxing inside her, he rolled her onto her right side, grabbed her left wrist, and sank his fangs in.

Her violent screams of death filled the empty house while her blood filled his mouth. Then all was quiet, and he left. It was time to hunt down his brother and his whore.

Devin and Salena were back in New Orleans, and she insisted on going by her house to inspect the damage and get cleaned up. The ruins made her burst into tears, and that made Devin even angrier with Gabriel for causing his love pain. As soon as she was washed up and dressed, he tried to lead her away from the mess. When they stepped back outside, though, an ambulance and two police cars pulled up to her neighbors' house. One of the officers was Ann Marx, who'd helped Salena before, and she noticed the damage done to her property. The other police entered the neighbors', while Officer Marx approached Salena.

"Miss Saunders, did you report this break-in? I don't think I've heard anything about it, and your other cases are still open," she said.

Salena was sure she was blushing. "I just got home from um"—she looked at Devin—"from a trip. So, I just now saw it. What's wrong with the Robertsons?"

Officer Marx looked at her note pad. "We got a disturbance call from the neighbor on the other side of them. I don't know what happened yet."

Salena and Devin both saw a gurney with a body bag exiting the house while another was being wheeled from the shrubs. A male officer yelled to Officer Marx, "We got a double here." Salena didn't need to have that explained—her poor neighbors.

Officer Marx went back to her interview with Salena, "Did you two see or hear anything from next door?"

Devin answered, "No ma'am. Just as she said, we returned from a camping trip only a few minutes ago. We didn't even notice their door was broken down, or we would have called you ourselves. We were ready to report the break-in on Salena's house when you pulled up." He gave her a tight smile, concealing his fangs.

Officer Marx looked up at the gorgeous mountain of man. "And your name is?"

Devin looked evenly at the police officer. "I am Salena's boyfriend, Devin Antonescu." He spelled it out for her.

"That's an interesting last name. What nationality is that?" the officer inquired, and Salena wondered too. She didn't even know he had a last name.

"It's Romanian, officer. My family came here from Romania many decades ago."

Turning back to Salena, who'd just been standing there quietly, the officer told her, "You need to come down to the station to file a report on your break-in. I'll make sure one of the officers here looks around first, okay?"

Salena just nodded and looked up at Devin for direction. He met her eyes, then told Officer Marx that he'd already checked the house, and no one was there. Then he excused himself and Salena from the officer's company, telling her they were going to go check into a motel. He promised they'd stop off at the station to file the report when she was over her shock.

Thankfully, the police left behind the ambulance and the coroner.

Salena looked up at Devin with tears in her eyes for her neighbors. "Do you think it was—" She didn't have to finish her sentence because he was nodding.

Gabriel had been at the neighbors' house too; he was sure of it. He'd already checked Salena's house and grounds, trying to sense his brother, before the police had shown up. Gabriel wasn't around anymore, but he might come back.

Salena looked around, remembering the cat. "Hey, I wonder what happened to my new furry friend. I haven't seen my new cat lately."

Devin nudged her and replied with his vampire grin, "Sure you have."

"What?" she asked before she understood the implication. "Are you saying that was you the whole time?" She flashed back to the wolves at Heloise's house and shuddered.

"Yes, it was always me. Vampires are shapeshifters too. I had to keep my eye on you to keep you safe, especially when my brother showed up, and when you went off into the ditch, I helped you out."

She'd completely forgotten about that. She now remembered feeling a tremor and then being mysteriously back on the road.

"So, what now?" she quietly asked.

Devin looked at her with a sexy grin. "Well, your bed is still intact, and I cleaned up some of the mess he'd made while you were in the shower.

She didn't need to know about the blood and urine on the floor of her bedroom. He touched her cheek lightly and leaned down to kiss her before scooping her up into his arms and carrying her to bed to make love to her. He felt sure she was finally coming around.

It was time to finish the battle. "Now, we head toward the ocean and wait for him to find us," Devin told Salena.

"But doesn't he know not to go there if that's where he could die?"

Devin shook his head to emphasize his words, "No, that was a secret the elder shared only with me. He knew it would come in handy someday. He knew Gabriel couldn't be trusted, even among his own kind."

"Well, I don't have my car and it's a long trip. My car is still at—" She didn't want to say it.

"I know you aren't ready to go back there, so we'll travel on foot." He took her hand and led her to the woods, so they wouldn't be seen. When he picked her up, she kissed him before snuggling against his brawny chest.

She knew they were headed for danger, so it was time to accept her destiny. If it was written in the stars, who was she to argue? She needed to come around to him before it was too late, and surprisingly, she was no longer afraid to. Something magical must have occurred to cause her sudden growing affection for him, but she couldn't deny it was there.

After the soft kiss, Devin took off running at breakneck speed because there was no time to waste. He headed toward Holly Beach where they would wait for Gabriel.

"Why do you want to be human again when you know you'll die someday?" she shouted over the pounding of his feet while he ran. "And how did you become a vampire to begin with?"

Devin slowed down to a walking pace, so he could talk. "I want to be mortal again because immortality pales in comparison to the love we will have. If you are lucky to find your soulmate, then you have found the one and only person to complete you. It's like a perfect glove; only one fits. That's the other reason I think you are Abigail reincarnated; you fit like a glove." He smiled down at her and winked.

Salena blushed at the implication, and she considered his words. She'd been foretold of her truelove by Heloise, Madame Zoyla, and Madame Marietta, and if he becomes human again, she'll be with her soulmate, and of course, that would be wonderful. But first, they had to survive his brother.

"Now, I'll answer your question about how I became a vampire. I was bitten by a female vampire back in Romania in 1330 when I was twenty-eight. After she bit me and drained my body considerably, she fed me some of her blood. That's how I transitioned."

Salena grimaced. "Did you have a wife or children at the time?" Out of jealousy, she was hoping he'd say no.

"I had never been married, which was unusual at the time, but I'd never found my perfect mate. I'd never

found the one I wanted to spend my life with until Ab—"
he caught himself. "—until you."

"You can say her name, Devin. I know she was
your first love." She felt jealous pangs, though. "Can't
vampires hook up with other vampires? Did you try to with
the girl who bit you?"

Devin chuckled, "I think you've watched too many
Twilight movies. It's not really like that. We don't pair off,
and we don't live together. If a vampire takes a mate, it's a
mortal one, and even that is extremely rare. To my
knowledge, I was only the second vampire to find my
soulmate and have the chance for mortality again. So, you
see, our love is unique."

Feeling uncomfortable about the last comment he
made, she felt like she had to explain. She looked up into
his violet-tinted eyes. "I'm not sure of what I'm feeling
right now. I'm not afraid of you anymore, but I've been
closed off to love for some time now, and this is all quite
bizarre. I'm open to being with you, but I need time to
develop my feelings.

"Today, I felt genuine concern when you were hurt,
and then it was about sex. That first time with you was
great, even though I was under a spell"—she shot him an
icy glare—"I just wanted that again without being
hypnotized. I wanted to enjoy it on my terms. And I admit
that something has changed, and that I am feeling *something*,
but I'm not ready to say that I'm in love with you. It would
be easier to accept my fate—as it has been laid out for me
over the past week—than to fight it, but I still don't know
what I'm feeling. At least not yet. Can we just date and let
it happen naturally?"

Devin heard her words loud and clear, but they
were just words. He knew there had been a change. He felt
it when they made love. And if his eyes were changing
colors, then it had to be true. He just had to wait for her to

realize it. She would come around. She had to because Abigail was still there inside her.

"Sure, we'll date," he told her with a wink.

Suddenly, a breeze blew past them, and it carried Gabriel's scent. It was time. He couldn't run away; he had to fight while he still could. Grabbing Salena's hand, he told her, "We must get closer to the water. Gabriel is near."

Devin and Salena finished their journey to the Gulf of Mexico. He'd chosen Holly Beach as their place to wait because it was the least populated by tourists and locals. He didn't want any witnesses to the battle. His main concern, though, was to keep Salena safe, even if he died in the process.

Salena was more nervous than she had ever been in her entire life. She was worried about Gabriel hurting Devin, of course, but she was also worried that she would hurt him. What if she couldn't be the person he expected her to be and already thought her to be? What if she couldn't be Abigail for him? Of course, she was also worried about what Gabriel would do to her if Devin failed. She'd felt his wrath once; she didn't dare think about the second time.

Devin kept an eye out for Gabriel. He could be anything—a stray dog walking by, a bird perched in a tree, a squirrel, or even just an insect. He could also show up in his human form, and Devin wasn't sure what would be worse. He knew Gabriel was strong, but he didn't know if his brother had any new tricks. He couldn't be sure of what to expect, so he decided to expect anything and everything.

The couple stopped and sat on the shore close to the water and waited. They didn't have to wait long.

74

Gabriel found the happy couple sitting on the beach. He wasn't sure if they were waiting for him or not, but it really didn't matter; he was ready. Salena looked to be healed nicely from his attack on her, which he found interesting. Devin must have remembered some spells from the old world, or maybe he had some new ones. Either way, it didn't matter. They were both good as dead. In fact, as he sniffed the air, he noticed a change in Devin's scent. Could it be? A wicked grin graced his gorgeous face, and a low chuckle escaped his throat. Maybe Devin was transitioning back to mankind. It was going to be too easy. Not only would Devin not be able to protect Salena, he wouldn't even be able to protect himself.

Gabriel waited until dusk before he made his move. The visitors in the area had gone on home or to dinner, which was good. He didn't want a lot of spectators for the show that was about to take place. A few he didn't mind—he would just kill them next. A huge crowd, though, could be a problem—even in good ole New Orleans.

He was close enough to Devin and Salena to watch them while the sun set without them noticing him. At least as far as he could tell, he hadn't been noticed. He knew Devin was on the lookout, though, but his brother's senses weren't as keen, especially if he was transitioning back to mortality.

He kept an eye on Salena as well. She had just recovered too quickly from his attack. He would not make that mistake again. He would make sure she *really* suffered next time. The thought of it made his fangs ache. It also put him into action. It was time.

He approached the couple as they sat on the beach, talking quietly. Maybe Devin was talking about the good old days and Abigail again. Gabriel thought, *If I were you, Salena, I wouldn't want to be compared to a ghost.*

Devin looked casually over his shoulder; he knew Gabriel was behind them. He gave Salena a squeeze and a kiss on the top of her head, and then he turned and lunged. Gabriel was fast, though, so Devin missed him for the most part. He was able to hit Gabriel's shoulder, however, which knocked him off balance for a split second. Gabriel lunged back, knocking Devin to the ground. They rolled around snarling, growling, and thrashing like a couple of starving bears.

Salena stood nearby, watching in horror as the vampire she was supposed to love tried to save her from the vampire she feared the most. And, of course, she knew what would happen to her if Devin lost; yet, she couldn't leave his side. So, she just watched, cried, and hoped. Then she saw blood, but she didn't know whose it was, and that really terrified her.

Gabriel had bit Devin in between his shoulder and his neck and ripped some flesh away, causing blood to splatter into the night.

Devin snarled and yelped in pain. Then he bucked his brother off him and rolled him over, putting himself on top. He delivered a crushing punch to Gabriel's chin while his other hand twisted Gabriel's right arm, trying to dislocate it. He didn't even know that it was the arm Salena had hurt in the car door.

Gabriel felt his injury reopen in his right arm from where that bitch had slammed the car door shut. He howled in pain from his injuries while delivering a blow to Devin's back with his knee. He was pretty sure he heard a bone break, and if he was lucky, maybe even two broke.

While rolling around on the sand with Devin, Gabriel eyed the bigger prize, Salena, who was standing there weeping—all alone and defenseless again. Devin was a total fool for bringing her with him; not that he wouldn't have hunted her down after killing his brother. But still, why bring the feast to the lion? With all his might, he flung Devin off him and scrambled toward Salena, who could only stand there in shock as he approached her.

Salena's legs were frozen in fear. She saw the vampire charging her, but she couldn't move for anything—just like in her dream, she was stuck in the mud. She couldn't even scream.

Devin felt a crushing blow to his back from Gabriel and had the wind knocked out of him when he was thrown off. He was sure he had a broken bone, too. It took him a mere second to regain his wits, even though he was not as strong as he once was, and he immediately realized Gabriel was headed toward Salena. Clambering after his brother, he rushed to save her.

Gabriel knew Devin was right behind him, and just as he got to the scared stiff Salena, he turned in a surprise move and faced Devin head on. The vampires lunged at the same time, and their bodies crashed into one another with a colossal force that knocked them both backward. Both lunged again, and Gabriel made contact with his fangs—they penetrated Devin's throat. He was about to deliver his final blow when Salena rushed to her lover's side. It astonished Gabriel enough to pause him from his attack, which was enough time for Devin to lurch upward and elbow him in his injured jaw, diverting his fangs from inflicting further damage.

Devin rolled away, but he knew it was over. Gabriel only had to attack him one more time, and it would be finished—and he would have failed his truelove again. He was just too weak. Even though the transition wasn't complete, it had started.

As he lay there panting for breath, with blood gurgling in his throat, he felt something else besides the pain. He felt his heart swell and a warm glow as he saw a look in Salena's eyes that had never been there before. It was a look he recognized from Abigail's eyes—it was love. And then he felt the most truly miraculous thing of all—he felt human. And as Salena leaned down and kissed his bloody lips, he was glad he would die in the arms of his soulmate; he was glad he could finally rest in peace.

Gabriel chuckled cruelly as he slowly approached the couple. "I have a confession for you, Brother. I am the reason Abigail was burned. I am the one who cried *witch*."

Gabriel lunged toward Devin for the final blow; he knew it was over. Just as he was almost on top of his dying brother, though, Salena blocked the attack with her body and quickly turned to stare into his shocked eyes before ripping into his throat. Then she picked him up with a strength she never had before and threw his body into the ocean.

Salena looked at her soulmate through raven-black eyes and with blood on her lips. "Now, what were those ingredients for that healing spell?" she asked with a vampire grin.

Please review:

Amazon: Author.to/AlexisKennedy
BookBub: https://goo.gl/7oqtxY
GoodReads: https://goo.gl/dGDFgo

Visit Alexis's website:
https://bit.ly/2wxAQ20

- ♥ Leave a comment
- ♥ Watch trailers
- ♥ See what's coming next
- ♥ Check out reviews
- ♥ Check out the blog
- ♥ Sign up for her newsletter

Thanks for your continued support!

Turn the page for a preview of Under the Blood Moon

Chapter 1

April 8, 2014
San Francisco, California

An earthquake shook the building and rattled the windows. Julia Stevens scampered out of bed, grabbing Oscar along the way, and rushed into the kitchen to hide under the table.

They both trembled in fear until it was over about twenty seconds, which felt like minutes, later. It hadn't been that strong, but it was frightening nonetheless. It was during those times that Julia was extra grateful to have Oscar by her side. He must have been grateful, too, because he licked her face before trotting back to bed. She followed right behind the dog; she had only an hour and a half yet to sleep before getting up for work.

Meanwhile, seven miles away in a hidden cavern, amber eyes slowly opened for the first time in two hundred years.

Julia tapped her fingers impatiently on the bar. Melanie always behaved this way—invite her out and then latch on to the first guy who flashed her a smile. Julia was not a prude by any means—she was all for the occasional hook-up—but at least she was picky. She flipped her long blond hair over her shoulder and downed her drink. Then she tapped her empty glass to get the cute bartender's attention—he was worth taking home. While waiting for her drink, she looked around the new club, Howl, to find Mel or at least someone decent to look at. There were a couple of hotties on the dance floor, but they were rubbing up against their dates. Sometimes, she'd flirt with them anyway by flashing her bedroom eyes, but she wasn't feeling sexy that night. In fact, she wished she'd just stayed home; Oscar was the only company she needed.

She turned back to the bar to have one last sip before leaving when a hand casually placed itself on her ass. She turned to slap the rude individual, but her hand stopped when she turned right into a broad chest. She was in four-inch heels, standing at six feet tall, yet she was only to the pecs on the man. She looked up into a chiseled face and eyes so deep brown that they were almost black. He was a hunk for sure, but Julia liked to be in charge. She didn't like men who thought they could take liberties with her, no matter how attractive they were. She looked the hunk right in his dark eyes.

"I think you have misplaced your hand, and I suggest you remove it," she hissed.

He leaned down, giving her a nice whiff of his musky cologne, and whispered in a husky voice, "What are you going to do about it?"

"This," she said as she brought her knee up to his nuts. He stopped her, though, with a reflex faster than a cat's, and he held her bare knee, stroking it gently with his thumb.

He leaned in again and whispered, "What else you got?" He released her knee but ran his hand up her thigh until it rested on her slender waist.

"You are way too forward," she spat at him and tried to shove him away, but he was like a brick wall and didn't budge.

He grinned a sexy, mischievous grin at her and cockily replied, "I think you like it."

The truth was, she did, but she wasn't going to tell him that. She pushed his hand off her hip instead and stepped aside, causing the other to fall away too. She knew, though, if he'd wanted to keep his grasp on her, he easily could have, and she felt almost insulted that he hadn't. She grabbed her clutch and turned to leave the club, not really caring how Mel got home anymore. As she stepped away, she thought she heard a low growl, and she almost turned around to look back. Almost.